ADVANCE PRAISE FOR THE IGUANAS OF HEAT

"Energy" writes Blake, "is eternal delight." Its repression is hell. From Iguanas: "what she was trying to force out of herself by straining, was hatred... burning her up...." Not "hatred of anyone or anything in particular, her husband or white people, but simply an inexhaustible source of energy." So with all of Yuriy Tarnawsky's writings, out of which emanate the ever-inexhaustible source of [human] energy, so with Yuriy Tarnawsky's poetry/fiction readings that radiate with that "inexhaustible source of [a writer's] energy"; so in my friendship with Yuriy Tarnawsky, where I have come to know his own "inexhaustible source of [Tarnawsky] energy." Iguanas screams its way wildly into hell, absent Blake's "delight." As we read on, we know that we, with Blake, might rescue ourselves from there, if we will.

> —Martin Nakell, author of *Monk* and *The Desert Poems of Southern California*

Yuriy Tarnawsky's *The Iguanas of Heat* is a haunting, magical novel that seduces and mesmerizes. Here, memories are like hot colors with a deceptively cool undertow that draws us out into an existential sea.

> —Derek Pell, author of *Naked Lunch at Tiffany's* and *What is Art?*

YURIY TARNAWSKY

THE IGUANAS OF HEAT

A NOVEL

2019

Cover Design by Norman Conquest
Cover Photo by David Clode
Author Photo by Oleh Holovackij

ISBN 1-884097-84-7
ISBN-13 978-1-884097-84-3

ISSN 1084-547X

This volume is volume 84 of
The Journal of Experimental Fiction

JEF Books/Depth Charge Publishing
Aurora, Illinois

JEF Books/Depth Charge Publishing
The Foremost in Innovative Fiction
Experimentalfiction.com

JEF Books are distributed
to the book trade by SPD: Small Press Distribution
and to the academic journal market by EBSCO

THE IGUANAS OF HEAT

A NOVEL

PART ONE

1

They were going to Mexico on vacation and their friends the Kaufmanns had been there the year before and were showing them the pictures of their trip so that they'd have a better idea what to expect.

The room was dark, illuminated only by the image on the screen and the traces of light that had managed to escape out of the projector.

The slide changed and it got darker. The picture showed a vast black space with dim smudges of gray on top and the left and thin uneven white lines like tendrils of plants searching for nourishment reaching downward from above and ending, some sooner, others later, in the black void, but never more than about halfway down the picture. But no, a few of the thicker ones did go all the way down, being cut off by the lower edge of the slide.

That's the cenote the driver took us to, El Pozo del Diablo—The Devil's Well—Walter Kaufmann said. It's in a cave and you get to it through a hole on top, and it's real deep, maybe fifty feet below the ground.

More like a hundred, Ginny corrected her husband. The driver said thirty meters.

You're right, Walter Kaufmann said. He did say thirty meters, which is about a hundred feet. It's deeper than all the others in the area and much more dangerous. The hole you get to it through is on a hillock, so it's further down to the water. The other ones, he said, are usually about fifty feet deep—fifteen meters. If you fall down, you're unlikely to survive.

Still some people do go swimming there, he continued. They climb down on the roots of the trees that reach all the way down to the water and along ropes that have been attached to the walls.

And the steps hewn out in the rock, Ginny said.

And the steps hewn out in the rock, he picked up her words. And they swim there. There're ledges down there on the bottom above the water and you can rest on them.

But not many people do it because it's in the country, far away from villages, he went on. Mostly adults. You have to drive to get there... in a car or a motorbike. In the cenotes close to villages everyone goes swimming. Adults and children.

You have to be real careful when you're there, Ginny took over. There're no protective barriers around the edge and the ground underfoot is slippery from the humidity, so it's easy to slip. And if you fall, you're gone.

The driver said, the year before somebody fell and drowned, Walter Kaufmann said. A tourist.

A visitor to the area, not a local, Ginny corrected him. Came with friends, was jostled, slipped, and fell. They pulled his body out, but it was too late. There was talk he was pushed because of an altercation or something and an investigation was started, but then was dropped and the whole thing was forgotten.

That's Mexico, Walter Kaufmann commented. Here you couldn't get away with something like that. Although I'm not sure if there was anything nefarious going on there. The driver said it was rumors.

Something akin to an explosion took place inside her, making her hear just disjointed words instead of sentences, "Jostled, slipped, fell, pulled out, body, too late, pushed, investigation, dropped, forgotten." This was the chance she'd been waiting for all these years! More than twenty! Since before they got married! Since their first date! When he drove her in his TR-3 to a secluded spot on the beach on the Cape and took her in the lee of a dune, which offered her body to him in the hollow of its huge white hand.

She will make him take her there, will jostle, no, openly push him, so that he'll finally know how she felt about him and will carry the knowledge with him to the water and preserve it forever in his memory, to stay with him for eternity in his death.

But what about the driver? What if he sees she'd pushed him and reports her to the police and testifies against her?

That's no problem. She will give herself to him to keep him silent. He'll agree to that for sure. He'll have an American woman, a white woman, for nothing. A woman who looks white. All nonwhites want to have a white woman. A status symbol. Retribution for centuries of exploitation, humiliation, colonization. She'll even offer him money if he wants some.

She pushed the thought of money out of her mind. It interfered with the train of thoughts she had planned out. She giving herself to him. He taking her. Right there on the slippery ledge. Or no, it'd be too dangerous. Outside, in the grass by the side of the road. His strong animal smell, sweat and male hormones, the salty, urinous taste of his penis in her mouth. He'll definitely want her to do it. She used to deny it to her husband because she didn't like it but will do it for him. Not only to keep him silent, but to please him, to let her husband understand how she felt about him if he were able to see it. To pay him back for all these years, all those times she had sex with him without wanting it, hating every second of it....

But how will she find the driver? She interrupted her thoughts. The Kaufmanns said they'd found him by accident and that nobody knew about this cenote.

Her euphoria vanished in an instant. She couldn't celebrate yet. She had some work to do. Had to find out more about the driver. Get his name.

A click was heard and a new slide appeared on the screen but she didn't see what it showed.

What was the driver's name? She asked in a voice she barely recognized as her own, unable to overcome the fear that had sprung up in her, hollowing out her inside. We'd like to see it when we're there.

I think it was Nicolas, Walter Kaufmann said. Nick. That's what he told us to call him.

No, it wasn't Nicolas, Ginny said. It was something else... Spanish. He told us to call him Nick, but it was.... Wait, she hesitated.... Nicanor. Nicanor was his name, but he said we could call him Nick.

That's right, her husband said. It was Nicanor.

And his last name? She pushed on, her heart now up in her throat, although emboldened with the progress she was making. Did you get it?

He never told us his last name, Ginny said. Taxi drivers usually don't. But if you ask around among the drivers at that market you should be able to find him. Pick him out of the other Nicanors.

She relaxed. True. Ginny was right. She could pick him out of the other Nicanor drivers. She wouldn't even have to ask about the cenote, but would recognize him. They'd just showed a picture of him—his face distended in a grin, his black eyes and white teeth shining.... She thought she remembered how the rest of his face looked but there was a jumble of disjointed features in place instead. She had to see it again, to memorize it.

Could you show his picture again? She asked in her normal voice, now fully composed. I would like to better see what he looks like so that I'll be able to recognize him.

The projector clicked twice and the man's face appeared on the screen again—faintly Japanese-looking, like a crude, rough-hewn, unattractive Toshiro Mifune, with jet black hair bristling at the temples, high cheekbones, black narrow eyes, and teeth with tobacco-stains on them in the wide-open, grinning mouth.

She felt his strong arms gripping her painfully, the overpowering smell of his sweaty man's body in her nostrils, the revolting flavor of tobacco and stomach acid in his breath and saliva in her mouth. Amazingly, she found it exciting and felt herself getting wet between the legs. She even thought she sensed the faint steering of the onset of an orgasm somewhere deep inside her. But she stopped herself once again. She mustn't get carried away. She wasn't there yet and should return to the present.

Full of smell and taste unlike her bland, insipid husband, she thought and with a mixture of hatred and disgust turned her head right and saw him sitting a few feet away, staring blithely ahead, unaware of the plans she'd made for him, slumped in the armchair like a giant white caterpillar, a huge noodle of toothpaste squeezed out of a Claes Oldenburg tube.

Will he be surprised!

She felt proud of herself—Red Maureen!

2

———

He came down from Dartmouth in his TR-3 to pick her up at Wellesley, having left home at dawn because he was there before breakfast and they had it together at the school cafeteria, and then they drove all the way to Cape Cod past Dennis and Orleans, and then up north, her hair and head messed up by the wind, the dunes splashing up on the right like white waves with the pale green spray of dune grass along their edges blowing in the wind, obscuring the huge blue friendly smile of the ocean, and then somewhere halfway up to Provincetown suddenly pulled off the highway onto an unpaved road on the right, toward the water, on the spur of the moment, clearly not having planned it as the car nearly flipped over, having driven like mad for what must have been two-three hours, not going any particular place, just to be away, away from himself, from his fear, his fear of her, fear of what he wanted to do, it was clear what he wanted to do, he timidly moving his hand toward her all the time, putting it close to her on the ridge between their seats next to the gearstick for her to touch, she deliberately not doing it, letting him be unsure, suffer, but having resigned herself to what would come, first date, but what the hell, why not, Dartmouth, six foot four, TR-3, a good catch, the road petered out into pools of sand, he drove the car in deep between the dunes, unseen from the highway, took her in the hollow of one which offered her to him in its giant cupped hand as if it owned her, was surprised there was no blood, she had to pacify him saying some women don't have a hymen, which he accepted, but with doubt, because he would return to the topic over and over, over the years, asking if she'd lied to him them, she replying calmly, why would she lie, she would have told him if she'd been with another man before, what's such a big deal, hers she partly broke with the handle of the hairbrush she sometimes gave herself pleasure with and the rest was taken by that southern Geowgia peaches, oh, Danny boy, who fed her mint julep after mint julep until she wasn't there, until she came back to throw up when it was over, funny, he ordered them mint juleps too afterwards, when they stopped off for lunch at some roadside bar-restaurant on the way back, as if he'd talked to oh, Danny boy, as if it was a common strategy among Ivy League College guys—oh, Danny boy attended Brown—who planned to seduce on their first date Seven Sisters College girls to feed the latter mint juleps except he did it bass-ackwards—first seduction, and then mint juleps, instead of the other way around.

He—bland, white like toothpaste squeezed out of a tube, his white underwear pure white, without a stain or odor, always pure white, then and now, then as always in a rush, no foreplay, kissing, just to get inside, men are like that, girls in college used to say, all they want is get inside you, squirm around for a minute or two like a dog trying to make itself comfortable before sleeping, make a mess, and leave. They don't know how to kiss. With Paula—Paul—it was different, when they were in High School and she'd come over after classes and they'd lock themselves in in her room and practice French kissing for hours, sitting on the edge of her soft bed, turned toward each other, first one playing the leading role, then the other, supporting the other one's back with her hand, holding firmly the other one's chin in the other one, her own tongue in the other one's mouth, probing, exploring, the window wide open into the yard onto the white picket fence cutting through the middle of it overgrown with sweet peas her mother had put up for that purpose, the tall wall of cottonwood trees in the background, Paul's—Paula's—saliva, hers undoubtedly too, sweet like the sweet peas they saw, as if inspired by them as their eyes roamed outside, bored, having nothing to do while their tongues were busy exploring.

They'd have to go into the bathroom afterwards to wash up down there, wet with excitement.

She's married now too, with two kids, girls, living back there, her husband a manager at the huge hardware store, looks even more like a man, the Portuguese face bony, the dissymmetry of the two sides of the lower jaw more pronounced than ever, the huge black eyes staring sadly out of the chalk-white face from under the thick black man's eyebrows under the closely cropped thick black hair.

They no longer call each other anymore or write, subdued, vanquished by the everyday stupor of married life.

3

That time when Bertie died, at the age of 98, and they were at her parents' for the summer, and she couldn't stop mourning her, for she had never married, had no family of her own, and was more than a second grandmother to her, her real Oma, whom she'd never seen, but more like second mother, her true mother, for she never got along with her real mother, never had one, as she lived like a spider shut up in her dark room, the double curtains always drawn, sitting in her bed propped up by pillows, guarding the dead flies of stock certificates, and bars of gold, and collections of gold coins and stamps, and boxes of jewelry laid out before her, caught in the spider web of her mind, or even more than that, like her older sister, a sister she'd always wanted but never had, her own soft, warm mirror image she could press her cheek to and stay that way for as long as she needed, she and her husband went over to the old house on the other side of the tracks, opened it up, went inside, and went through the dark rooms, the floorboards creaking under their feet, the musty smell of the stale warm air in their nostrils, and she began to cry, remembering Bertie, how she would take her there as a child, when she'd come down from her place in the city and tell her stories about her family, her Oma and Opa, and of her father, and his brother and sister when they were little, and who and what was in the picture on the wall, and when this piece of furniture was bought and when that one, and where did this lamp on the table or the ceiling or that rug on the floor come from, and as they were in her grandparents' bedroom and she lay down on the huge four-poster bed, big like a hill with the featherbed on it under a dark green, faded velvet spread, from which she'd sprung, her grandmother giving birth to her father on it, on which he'd likely been begotten, crying, tears like a sheet of cellophane covering her face, he lay down on top of her, and put his hand down, and under her skirt, reaching up for the top of her panties, she knew what he had in mind, let him do it, it'll make her feel worse, appropriate, make the tears flow more freely, helped him do it by raising up her hips, he pushed up her skirt, was on top of her in seconds, penetrated, she moist there, moist with tears, went on uncharacteristically for a long time, in and out, in and out, raised himself up on his arms after a while, looked down, would bend down from time to time to give her a peck on her lips, cheeks, eyes, forehead, as if kissing a bouquet of wilted, withered, dry roses wrapped in cellophane, a freight train rumbled by along the tracks that ran just yards away, shaking the house, bed, her, him, everything creaked, rattled, tinkled, he finished just then, so feebly you couldn't tell, she didn't know it, pushed him off herself when she realized he'd finished, when he stopped moving, lying still on top of her like a bundle of wilted weeds on her grave, she got off the big bed, straightened herself up, walked like a sleepwalker through the huge house, room to room, sobbing, he behind her like her shadow, meek, guilty, her panties in his fist, tried to give them to her, she chasing his hand away like a big bothersome fly, a gadfly, tried to apologize for his action, saying he thought it'd help, he was sorry, life is like that, death is part of life, you have to accept it, live it, it's a daily struggle, struggle every hour, minute, second, building, constructing yourself, existence precedes essence, tried to kiss, embrace her by the huge lilac bush growing at the corner of the house outside, she resisting, succeeding, stiff, prickly, like a lilac bush gone wild, a bush green but not in bloom, they didn't talk to each other until dinnertime, at the table, it was impossible not to with her parents there, it was bad the rest of the summer, remnants staying on all the way East, lasting on, to this day, forever.

4

Existentialism, sickness onto death, the sickness of the white man, pale-bodied, pale-faced, sitting bent over a half-empty cup of cold black coffee in a dark café, staring blankly into nowhere, their first time in Paris, when he was working on his book on Existentialism, they went to its cathedral, the Sartre Chartres, *Les Deux Magots*, to inhale the air, aura of the place, movement, vaguely hoping to see Sartre and Beauvoir, sure they wouldn't, people that important don't mingle with the mortals, open themselves to so much risk, hopes don't come true, but then, ten minutes after they'd sat down, ordered coffee, lo and behold, who wouldn't stride in through the door if not Sartre, not with Beauvoir, but with a bevy of young boys and girls, mostly girls, students, dancing around him like angels around God, he cut a weird figure, almost a midget, in rumpled clothes, shirt, the tie—a limp rope dangling from his neck, hair greasy, not washed for days, maybe weeks, thin on top, slicked over, skull shining through, one eye behind the round glasses weird, white, big, pointing to the side, like a gut sticking out of the eye socket, she whispered to him he should go over, introduce himself, tell the great man about his book, he wouldn't, shook his head, started shaking, asked her not to bother him, leave him alone, stared blankly into nowhere, a cowardly pale-bodied, pale-faced white man, not brave, not like those bare-chested, bare-legged, red-skinned braves, their heads crowned with eagle feathers, no, sprouting mighty feather manes like fierce lions of the sky, cheeks marked with red and white clay, galloping madly atop their horses, bareback, reinless, legs giving directions by pressing down on the hot, sweaty, bulging sides, tomahawks, bows and arrows, short Winchester rifles in their hands, waving them menacingly, mouths emitting endless streams of frightening high-pitched la-la-la-la sounds, galloping to do battle, battle with the white man, the taker of their land, usurper of their rights, to kill him, take their land back, galloping precedes the white man's death, galloping toward her, to join her, make her join them, her brothers, her people, they said she was white, *echt Deutsch*, pure German, her grandfather, Opa, Kasper Kraus came from Pomerania, homesteaded, did well, sent for his sweetheart Katarina, she came, they married, had children, got rich, brought her younger sister Berta over, there was an Indian hand around the ranch, a big, strapping, good-looking guy everybody liked, after Kasper Jr. and Charlotte there were no children for a long time, almost ten years, then her father Karl came, looked a little like his father Kasper but also Indian, high cheekbones, tall, Kasper was short, people joked he had two fathers, Kasper and the Indian, they said Kasper turned sterile, wanted more children, and asked for the Indian to help out, Katarina liked him a lot, they took turns, first Kasper, then the Indian, so the semen was mixed, people joked, but she thought it was possible, likely the Indian was involved, it was true there was something Indian about the way Kasper looked, so maybe that's why her father looked a little Indian, but maybe not, maybe because of the Indian, the Indian died of tuberculosis a few years later, there were no more children, her mother was of German origin too, beer makers from Milwaukee, called Kieselbach, her father met her when in college, at Marquette, so supposedly she was pure German, but she looked a little Indian like her father, looked part Indian, but inside was a full-blood, Indian through and through, daydreamed about being one, years ago there was an Indian woman who led the braves in her village to fight the settlers who'd attacked them after the chief was killed and they won, it was her, she'd reveal herself one day and lead her people to fight the whites.

5

And then there was that big hullabaloo, *viel Lärm um nichts*, much ado about nothing when her husband had transferred to Harvard to work on his PhD, and they were living in Cambridge, and she bought herself a palomino she called Geronimo with money from the trust Opa Kraus had set up for her, and had it stabled at Hobson Stables where she helped out with grooming the horses and exercising them for Geronimo being stabled there for free and for her to get paid a little in addition to augment her husband's meager fellowship stipend which barely covered their food and rent, since they didn't want to deplete her trust or take handouts by either of their parents, and one day as they were practicing jumping the horse fell down and broke its leg, and she had it put away because it was suffering too much and it would have cost a fortune to keep it alive, and it probably wouldn't have been any good if it pulled through anyway, and especially since she had it insured just for that reason, for what would have been the point in getting insurance if you weren't going to use it? If you knew from the beginning you weren't going to use it? Stupid! And she was able to get herself another horse with the money, a big beautiful chestnut she called

Crazy Horse as an homage to its predecessor Geronimo as well as to the great chief who was on equal footing with Geronimo in her Pantheon of Indian chiefs, and he, her husband, was all up in arms about it. How can you kill it? You used to say you loved it, and now you have it put away, to get the insurance money, and you get yourself another horse practically the next day with that insurance money, blood money, would you do the same with me? Have me put away when it would be a bother for you to take care of me? Is that what love means to you? An empty word? Nothing? Him she would, but that's another story, the two things were not the same, her father understood it, Indians would have understood it, Indians did understand it, do understand it, life, nature is cruel, old grass rots and new comes up green, a tree falls down and becomes food for a new one, you kill a buffalo and get strong from its meat, sire a big healthy son, Geronimo dies and Crazy Horse comes into being, one thing's death precedes another one's life, only whites sit in dark cafes over half-empty cups of cold black coffee, staring into nowhere, depressed that existence precedes essence.

6

_____

When she was still living with her parents, sometimes she was Ki'somma, a young Indian-looking man whose name meant "sun" in Indian. He was her parents' son, although it wasn't certain if by adoption or from a union between her mother and an Indian man because her father was sterile and had asked her mother to let herself be impregnated by an Indian. He wanted a son and was fond of Indians, being potentially half-Indian himself. The two possibilities coexisted peacefully in her mind, neither of them overcoming the other and she would choose either one or the other, whichever seemed appropriate at the moment. In spite of the situation, her father loved Ki'somma as his own son and the two were close. Her mother never figured in these musings and it was possible she was no longer there.

Ki'somma was tall and handsome, with pure Indian features—copper-colored skin, high cheekbones, black eyes, and straight long hair, and aside of her father—that is, his adopted father—had no friends in town or anywhere else. He couldn't feel close to white people and was estranged from his own. He didn't even know who they were or where they lived. He felt best around farm animals, especially horses, and loved the landscape around the town as something living. The gently curving hills covered with short grass around the town and the distant rocky, tree-covered mountains were like people he was friends with.

He being so handsome, all the girls in town had their eyes on him and hoped they could catch him. Ki'somma was indifferent to them however, both because they were white and because of what they expected of him. He wasn't interested in sex and the idea of marriage was not so much scary as foreign to him. He didn't understand why two people would want to live together and have children. Being around farm animals and communing with nature was all he ever wanted.

There was one girl in town who was in particular very keen on him. She came from a German family, was beautiful, tall and slender, with long blond hair and blue eyes, and was called Elise. People joked that the well-known Beethoven piano piece had been written for her. She played the piano and would often play it beautifully.

When she was around Ki'somma, she made it clear that she was interested in him and did all she could to have him fall for her. Her father and his were friends and she would often come over so as to be near him.

She'd wanted to learn horseback riding and her father made arrangements for Ki'somma to teach her. He even bought a horse and arranged for it to stay at his father's stable.

Being in close physical contact for a long time the two did get closer together and one day Elise managed to entice Ki'somma to have sex with her. He was not in love with her and his attitude toward marriage and sex hadn't changed but seeing how much the girl wanted him, in a moment of weakness, he gave in to her and did what she wanted. He regretted it as soon as it was over and swore he wouldn't do it again, but told himself what was done was done and decided not to dwell on it.

Unfortunately his act, as most in life, had a consequence and in his case the latter was monumental. Elise got pregnant and in a month or two found that out.

He was in a state of shock when she told him and in an instant his whole life was turned upside down. Horses and the beautiful landscape lost their meaning and he himself was no longer he, Ki'somma, but some stranger who'd come from somewhere and moved into his body.

Things around him were happening outside his control and he had a feeling he was learning about what was happening to him by reading about it in the newspaper. He didn't even try convincing Elise to have an abortion, partly because of knowing she wouldn't consent to it and partly because he himself found the idea abhorrent and eventually plans were made for the two of them to get married.

One day however, he found a solution to his quandary. He'd never entertained anything like this before, but it came to him in a flash and he realized with amazement that it was simple, easily achievable, and would accomplish exactly what he wanted. It was going to be like clearing the table of a mess of dirty dishes and remnants of food with one swipe of his hand.

A holiday was coming up and he suggested to Elise for the two of them to go for a ride in the mountains. He knew some beautiful places she'd never seen before and he would show them to her.

She agreed readily and when the day came they packed a picnic lunch, saddled the horses, and rode off into the mountains.

They rode for hours, climbing higher and higher, he pointing out to her various beautiful spots, and finally came to the place he had in mind—a rocky bluff over a precipice that went a couple of thousand feet down. They stopped their horses feet away from the edge and he pointed out to her how beautiful was the view stretching before them, saying that this was in particular what he wanted to show her. She replied that the vista was indeed magnificent and thanked him for having brought her there.

He said nothing in response but yelped a high-pitched Indian cry, nudged her horse with his, making it rear up and plunge into the emptiness before it.

7

The following scenario she would act out throughout her life however, into and during her marriage.

She's somewhere in high mountains, on a grassy slope with sharp rocky peaks towering all around her. The slope is steep and she can not only see it but also tell from the way her feet feel on the ground. Down below her, perhaps a hundred yards or so, there's a little square, single-storied hut with white walls and a steep shingled roof with long overhanging eaves as befits a house in the mountains. It looks vaguely like a Swiss chalet, so it's probably in the Alps rather than someplace else similar, for instance the Rockies.

She's come there in the capacity of a journalist to report on what will take place in the hut and so starts walking down toward it. There is no path, the ground is covered with sharp stones, and she has to tread carefully around them so as not to catch her toe on one of them and fall. The slope is so steep it might be dangerous. If she falls down, she might roll.

She gets down to the hut fine however, and steps inside. Its door has been left wide open, which seems to have been done for her benefit, to make her task easier.

There are windows in three of the walls, but inside it is dark. It must be due to the overhang of the eaves, which restrict the light coming in.

The wall without windows is on the left. There are cupboards on most of it and below them a gas stove with a sink next to it, and it is separated from the rest of the hut by a counter which has a few tall stools standing along it—in other words, this is the kitchen part of the hut. There is a long wooden table in the space to the right of the counter with matching chairs around it and a big bed without a headboard in the far corner on the right, covered with a thick red and black checkered blanket.

Two men are doing something behind the counter, walking back and forth and puttering around as if cleaning up after breakfast. This must be what they are doing because it feels early in the morning.

The men show no sign of acknowledging her appearance as she steps in as if she were invisible or someone who will be reporting on what they will do, for instance someone filming them, although she doesn't carry a camera. But her eyes and mind are sort of a camera, so that's probably why they are behaving in this fashion.

The men are tall and slender, athletic-looking, with short dark hair, one of them visibly older than the other—in his late forties or early fifties as compared to early twenties. They both wear identical heavy red and black checkered lumber jackets and from what she can tell by looking over the top of the counter, jeans and, judging by the sound their feet make on the floor, heavy boots.

The counter is all clear, so they must be about finished, and just then the older man turns away from the counter, opens the cupboard in front of him, pulls out a modern-looking crossbow and a quiver full of arrows, shuts the cupboard, and asks the younger man if he is done.

The latter stands with his back to the older man, holding a dish towel in his hands, drying them with it, and hearing the older man speak, turns around and says that he is.

Alright then, the older man says, they should go. It is getting late. Is he ready?

Yes, he is, says the younger man, swipes the towel a few more time over his hands, turns around, hangs it on the bar on the front of the stove, turns back again, and faces the older man.

Should he carry the crossbow? He asks.

Nooo, the older man says, he will do it himself, but then changes his mind and says, yes, it's heavy and he's a little tired, so let him carry it, and hands the weapon to the younger man. He himself will carry the quiver.

The younger man takes the crossbow in his hands with great care as something not only precious but also fragile in spite of how strong it looks, being made out of metal and glittering in the semi-darkness. He caresses it and looks at it lovingly before pressing it to his chest.

Does he have the right shirt on? The older man asks, and does it sit properly on his chest?

Yes, he does and it is, the younger man replies and opens wide his lumber jacket, revealing a black t-shirt with a red target printed on the left side of his chest, over his heart, consisting of a big red dot with two concentric circles around it.

He should make sure it sits properly when they are doing it, the older man says, this way there'll be less discomfort.

Yes, he will, the younger man says, he knows it. He will adjust it properly in time.

Alright then, the older man says, they should go, turns around and walks out from behind the counter, with the younger man following. He is pressing the crossbow to his chest and there is something like a trace of a smile on his lips.

They get out from behind the counter and walk toward the door, practically brushing against her but showing no sign of recognition she is there as if she were really invisible rather than ignoring her as someone making a film. She sees then to her satisfaction that the men are indeed dressed as she'd suspected—they wear jeans and heavy boots.

They step out the door and she follows them, watching them going up the slope in the direction from which she came.

She knows where they are going—to a sheltered, secluded spot among cliffs where the execution will take place, and she will follow them there.

8

She called it face-painting and started doing it on their honeymoon which they were spending on the Cape in Orleans.

They were staying at a little Bed and Breakfast place, a white two-storied private home on a hill, about a fifteen minutes' walk from the beach.

They'd come back in early afternoon from the beach, exhausted from the hot sun and frolicking in the waves, and wanted to rest up a little before going out to dinner later that evening.

The room they were staying in was on the corner and had spectacular views of the dunes and the gently curving beach stretching as far as the eye could see in both directions.

After taking a shower he lay down in his undershirt and shorts on top of the bed without unmaking it, directly over the bedspread, planning to take a short nap. Stirred up by the incredible vista of the deep blue sky, the nearly identical blue sea below it, and the white beach stretching into distance, its edge blinding bright in the sunlight like a freshly sharpened sword, as well as by the bright sunlight streaming into the room through the white curtains and lighting up the white interior, seeing her husband stretched out on his back with his eyes closed, she came up to the bed, sat down on its edge, and began running her fingers over his face, drawing an image inspired by what her eyes had just seen.

He wasn't asleep, but kept his eyes shut, letting her do it.

She started at the top, delineating his forehead, running the tips of her fingers along the edge of his hair. She then did a little dance with them above the line, representing the hair. Next she ran her hand flat over his forehead, smoothing it out, gently shaping its surface. After that she ran her fingers over his eyebrows, first one, then the other, transferring to them the slight curvature of the beach, but making it greater. She repeated both eyebrows a few times to make sure she got them right. She then did the eyes, feeling out their roundness under the eyelids, doing the eyelashes as a gentle tickling in the end. Then she moved over to his nose, drawing its long straight line a few times, and after that the little curves of the nostrils and the holes they formed. These she did by touching one of her fingers under his nose first on one side and then on the other. Then she sketched out the little shallow groove that ran from his nose to the top of his mouth by running one of her fingers along it. The mouth she did very carefully, first the upper lip with a slight dip in the middle and then the lower one as the mirror image of the upper but without the dip, the line between them, and finally the surfaces of the two lips, running the tips of her fingers over them a few times. She then drew the outline of his face down from the temple to the tip of the chin on one side and then from the tip of the chin up to the temple on the other. She corrected this next by putting a little dent at the tip of the chin she had missed. After that she drew his cheeks and the space under his eyes and other places she'd created by touching them gently with her hand.

At this point a faint smile had appeared on his lips and, noticing it, she drew it by ticking first one and then the other corner of his mouth.

All done, she looked at what she'd created and, liking it, bent down and placed her lips on his, making sure they fit properly.

9

She didn't feel like sleeping and since her husband did, she decided to leave him alone in the room while she went downstairs and got herself a cup of coffee.

There was another woman in the kitchen in addition to the hostess—the next-door neighbor whose name was Maureen. The two sat at the kitchen table, drinking coffee, the former in a chair at the head and the latter on the bench against the wall, and she was invited to sit with them, which she did in the chair across from the woman, facing her, after being poured a cup of coffee by the hostess.

From the very first moment she saw the woman she was smitten by her, not so much in the sense of being attracted, as in the original physical sense of the word—struck and overwhelmed.

The woman looked tall, sitting on the bench, and slender, with long black wavy hair, black, expressive eyes, and an elegant, chiseled face, wore a tight red sleeveless dress, and projected incredible vivacity and energy as if she was an actress on the stage, playing a particular role. Reminded of the Bizet character, at first she thought the woman should be called Carmen instead of Maureen, but within a few minutes the latter's personality imbued the name "Maureen" with all its qualities so that it felt proper and she continued feeling about it this way from then on.

She didn't follow the conversation and essentially had no idea what it was about—it dealt with something going on in the neighborhood and a couple of their mutual women friends— but was aware only of the woman's voice, the expressions on her face, and the gestures that accompanied her talking, as if she was at a concert, listening to a symphony played by an orchestra, being impacted by it but unable to understand.

The woman stayed only for a short time, perhaps ten minutes, and as she was going out the door she herself didn't even regret the former was leaving, as if feeling she had no right to place any demands on someone as outstanding as her, but felt blessed she'd had the opportunity to meet her. She felt their encounter had a dramatic impact on her and that she'd been changed by it forever. She was a new person now and would never again be the same as before.

The hostess went on to do things around the kitchen and not wanting to be in her way she decided to go back upstairs. She would sneak quietly into their room so as not to wake up her husband and sit in the armchair, reading a magazine she'd brought along until he woke up.

Walking up the stairs though, she became curious about how the change she'd undergone had affected her appearance. She was sure she looked different. The bathroom was just ahead on her right and she decided to step inside and see.

She went in, locked the door, turned on the light, quickly walked up to the wash basin, and bending over it, looked in the mirror.

She was shocked. Looking back at her was the same well-known, worn image of herself—the woman she and everybody else knew as Greta Kraus. Nothing about her had changed.

She was about to despair but a quiet, calming inside voice told her to be patient and she obeyed it, staying as she was, staring at herself intently eye to eye, waiting for something to happen.

She was straining while holding her breath and little by little her face began to turn red and swell up. Her eyes also kept bulging more and more out of her head until tears ran from them down her cheeks, and in the end she saw her new self, the changed Greta Kraus that was ready to take on the world— a dangerous-looking woman with a frightening swollen face named Red Maureen.

The physical reason for her appearance was straining, but the real cause of it, the core on top of which her new self sat and which is what she was trying to force out of herself by straining, was hatred—a boundless, indescribable hatred which was burning her up inside and wanted to come out at all cost. It wasn't hatred of anyone or anything in particular, her husband or white people for instance, but simply an inexhaustible source of energy which she had to unload onto something even if it was only whatever was at hand.

Originally, when still in the kitchen, she was going to call herself simply Maureen for the woman who'd helped her change, but as she looked at herself in the mirror she realized that "Red" was a necessary addition—for the woman's red dress, for her own presumed Indian heritage, for the color of her real face, and most of all for the color of blood, for how could you quench such hatred in anything other than blood?

So, as they were having dinner later that night, same as her husband, she ordered steak instead of fish she would have normally asked for, specifying for it to be served rare as compared to medium of her husband's, which she ate with lots of ketchup lathered over it, and to drink, a Bloody Mary instead of the usual gin and tonic which is what the two of them usually had.

When he remarked jokingly she'd turned communist, she explained in a matter of fact voice her periods had been getting heavy lately and she had read recently it was advisable for women in such situations to eat lots of tomatoes and red meat.

10

_____

Following is a dream she once had.

She's at her parents' home next to the big lilac bush by the old house. She's bent over and is coughing, as if trying to clear her throat from phlegm as when you have a cold. She can feel it's there but can't get it out. It's sticking to the roof in the back of her mouth like a piece of string, so to help herself she sticks her fingers in her mouth, grabs it, and pulls it out.

She hasn't pulled out all of it though because she can still feel it in her throat, so she pulls on it more and soon sees it in her fingers—a long uneven, greyish-white string, thicker at both ends and thinner in the middle like a piece of used chewing gum.

She grabs the end of it with her other hand and pulls on it now with both until her arms are fully extended, but the thing still doesn't break and keeps sticking in her throat.

She lets go of it, grabs it with both of her hands close to her lips, pulls on it, once more extends her arms all the way out, but it still doesn't break and sticks in her throat.

She continues pulling on the thing as before and letting it go and then grabbing it close to her lips and pulling again, and it gathers on the ground below her in a little gray mound.

Suddenly she notices that the last piece she has pulled out looks different. It is wider than it has been until then and there are dark spots in it, two of them, side by side.

She pulls more and a bigger dark spot appears further down, making the three look like a pair of deformed elongated eyes with a likewise deformed elongated mouth below them.

She keeps on pulling and two little appendages appear sticking out from the opposite sides of what she has pulled out, frilly on the end like tiny arms and hands. And after that there comes a pair of different appendages, looking like legs and feet.

She realizes then what's happening—there is a fetus inside her and she is trying to pull it out through her mouth.

Then something happens—her mouth and throat are full of something and she gags, waking up at that instant.

Feeling she will throw up any second, she jumped out of bed and in the darkness ran to the bathroom, lifted the lid on the toilet bowl, knelt down before it, and vomited.

She kept doing it over and over, eventually feeling something hot flowing down her thighs onto the floor at the same time.

When her husband rushed into the bathroom, turned on the light, and gave out a wild scream, she saw that she was kneeling in a pool of blood. She was having a miscarriage.

11

They came down to Newport for the second Oscar Peterson concert at the invitation of her husband's old Dartmouth chum Elliot, who came from a prominent Newport Brahmin family, and stayed at the latter's ancestral home. They missed the first concert and being big fans of Peterson's music were glad to be given an opportunity to see him play in person.

She remembered the giant violent orchids of sea waves breaking on the rocks at the nearby Bailey's Beach when they went swimming there in the morning, recovering from sitting for hours in hot sun in the dusty park at the concert while listening to music by lying stretched out full length in the huge bathtub filled with barely lukewarm water in the gleaming white bathroom that had fresh and salt water coming out of the faucets and was fitted out with gold-plated fixtures, and having cocktails before dinner in a crowd of guests decked out in white on the terrace in the back of the house.

There were probably a dozen guestrooms lined up along the corridor as in a hotel, some sharing a bathroom, others with a private one. The one in their room was private.

After a buffet dinner of salads, pâtés, and cold seafood served with champagne there was a classical music concert given by a young Hungarian pianist with the first name Attila, apparently a friend of a friend of the family. A big black grand piano was wheeled into the room from the conservatory, people made themselves comfortable in armchairs, regular chairs, on sofas, and the rug on the floor, and after a brief speech in which the pianist was introduced, the concert began.

Oscar Peterson's playing was amazing in that this huge corpulent man sat still as a rock in his chair, barely moving his arms, letting only his hands glide back and forth above the keyboard, causing his fingers to generate an endless flow of patterns of incredibly rapidly changing sounds by touching the keys below.

The concert was something completely different. She played the piano herself and had been to many piano concerts before but had never experiences anything similar. It was an all-Liszt program and it seemed the piano was a giant black bird chained to the floor which the pianist was relentlessly torturing, making it try to free itself by flapping its huge single wing while giving out continuous blood-curdling cries of anguish. These ranged from ear-piercing, high-pitched shrieks of pain, through deafening full-throat screams of outrage, to faint, barely audible pleas for mercy. It seemed the bird was the eagle in the ancient Greek legend that used to tear out the heart and liver of Prometheus as they kept growing back, as a punishment by gods for having brought fire to man, and it was now being paid back for what if once did. The avenger though wasn't Prometheus himself but someone from our times, a brave young man who took it upon himself to punish the wrongdoer.

The playing of each piece was rewarded with wild cheering and applause and when the concert was over people crowded around the pianist, eager to congratulate him and to get to know him better.

Like apparently virtually everyone else she was overwhelmed by the performance and stood in line to get to talk to the man and when she finally did, refused to give a chance to others who stood behind her to do the same. There weren't many of them left and as desert and coffee started to be served, seeing that their chances to talk to the man were slim at best, eventually they all went away and she and the man were left alone. She wound up spending much of the rest of the evening with him.

She seldom found men attractive but in this case the situation was different. There was something truly magnetic in the power the man's playing projected and in addition his name Attila evoked in her mind Attila the Hun, the destroyer of Rome, which made her think of him as a kindred spirit. Even if not an Indian, in her eyes he was a brave.

They talked about Hungary, Huns, American Indians, and, of course, music, and at one point she found herself feeling sentimental and asked him to play for her Beethoven's "For Elise." She liked the piece a lot and would play it sometimes herself when she had access to a piano. She'd left her piano at her parents' home when she got married and had essentially given up playing even though she was pretty good at it.

He played the piece extremely delicately, which was surprising after his muscular treatment of the Liszt pieces, and people liked it so much that he was forced to play it a second time at general insistence.

It had gotten to be very late by then and the playing turned out to be the conclusion to the evening.

12

_____

While talking to the man she noticed the angry looks her husband was giving her, circling around them like a hungry but cowardly wolf a prospective kill, afraid to come up. She was well aware of his jealous nature and normally would cave in to her fear of him and modify her behavior but this time decided she didn't care. Let whatever might happen, happen. She would handle it then. She was no longer afraid of him.

As was his custom he didn't say anything until they were in their room, in bed and with the lights out, and only then began berating her for her behavior. She'd acted like bitch in heat, sniffing the man and letting him sniff her. People's eyes were popping out of their heads in amazement as they watched the two of them talk and would shake their heads and turn away eventually, unable to stand the sight. He was burning up with shame inside all the time and didn't know where to hide. Time and again he would barely manage to stop himself from going up to them, grabbing her by her hair, and pulling her off like a cave man his misbehaving woman, which is what he should have done. And the worst thing was the man's playing for her "For Elise." That broke the camel's back, was a giveaway, proof she'd fallen in love with him and he with her. It was her favorite composition and she used to play it especially for him when she could, and now had another man play it for her in front of everyone. That was unbelievable. Like it was the end of their marriage. Was it? He didn't know how the two of them could stay together any longer....

She lay still, indifferent to his anger, not defending herself, making no attempt at explaining why she'd behaved as she did, and when, as she'd expected, eventually he switched over to accuse her for the umpteenth time of having lied to him about her virginity when they made love the first time, boiling mad with anger, she shouted that she had enough of that subject, that she'd explained it to him satisfactorily many times already and never wanted to hear about it again.

Without having planned to do it, on the spur of the moment, she jumped out of bed, ran to the bathroom, turned on the light, locked the door, ran up to the mirror, and stared at herself.

Looking back at her from the cramped glass prison cell of the mirror was the bland, familiar image of herself, and so as she had done that time on their honeymoon on Cape Cod in Orleans as well as on many other occasions standing in front of a mirror, she held her breath and started to strain, seeing her face gradually swell up and turn red and her eyes bulge out of her head more and more, feeling at the same time the hatred inside her grow stronger and stronger.

47

There was a soft knock on the door, his timid voice called out, Gretchen, Gretchen, and in response she said softly, as if to herself, Red Maureen, Red Maureen.

He continued knocking and calling her name and eventually, without turning away from the mirror and speaking loudly so that he could hear her, she told him to go back to bed. She was fine and would be out soon. She was merely feeling a bit queasy from having had too much to drink.

13

Following is another one of her dreams.

She's in some big dark space as on the stage in an empty theater, with a bright spotlight shining on her so that she can't see anything beyond it, and before her, perhaps four or five steps ahead, still in the spotlight, stands a little boy two or three years old, facing her, looking into her eyes. He has long flaxen hair, blue eyes, and fair skin, and is dressed in a little white and navy-blue sailor suit with short pants and a shirt with a big square collar in the back, and has white socks and white sandals on his feet. His eyes are sparkling like blue diamonds, and he is smiling ear to ear, reaching out with his hands toward her as if wanting her to pick him up and take him in her arms. It is her son and she thinks he is adorable and loves him beyond description. He is the only thing in her life that matters and she is boundlessly grateful for having him.

She bends down and reaching out with her arms and wiggling her fingers so as to entice him to move forward asks for him to come.

He doesn't do it however but giggles and makes a little step back instead. He's playing games.

She smiles herself and straightens up a little and steps forward, asking him to come.

In response he laughs out loud, and giggles some more, and makes a couple of steps backward, still keeping his arms stretched out, wanting her to go after him. The spotlight moves with him so that he stays in it.

She steps forward herself, reaching out with her arms once more, and says gently, No, no, no, and asks for him to come.

He laughs again however and steps back and she goes after him once more.

This is repeated a few more times and in the end she gets angry and shouts for him to stop, and since he doesn't, she runs toward him, aiming to grab him, but at that instant he leans back and starts falling, as if into an abyss.

She realizes then she's not on a theater stage but on the edge of a cliff high up in the mountains. Her son has stepped over the edge and is falling. She has lost him and will never get him back.

In despair she lets out a wild scream and jumps after him even though she can no longer see him.

She then woke up.

14

_____

This time they'd come down to New York City to spend the weekend with some friends.

They arrived Friday afternoon and went out for dinner at a restaurant later that night. Saturday, they spent the afternoon at the MoMA and in the evening attended a cookout on the roof of the building where their friends lived, to which a bunch of other people were invited.

The roof was flat, covered with tar and gravel and surround by a brick parapet about three feet tall, with a water tower in one corner and a rectangular bunker-like structure in the center with a door in it, which provided access to the stairwell. A whole bunch of TV antennas were set up on its roof, making it look like a crowded little cemetery full of decapitated crosses. A large area was set up next to the structure with tables and benches clustered around a grill and residents of the building were free to use it, provided they'd scheduled it with the management.

It was in the summer and the day was typical for that time of the year—uncomfortably warm and muggy, with an overcast sky that hung low over the city like an immense bed with its linen messed up after a night's sleeping, turned upside down. Miraculously the linen stayed attached to the bed and didn't fall down to smother the landscape beneath it.

They were grilling hamburgers and hot dogs and a cloud of blue smoke mixed with the smell of hot grease and burnt meat hung over the area where people were gathered, in particular those at the grill, doing the grilling—three or four of them, all men—who appeared to be so enthusiastic about what they were doing that it'd have been nearly impossible to tear them away from it even by force.

She'd been mingling with the other guests, chatting and sipping on her gin and tonic and as she accidentally turned her head one way saw her husband standing by himself far away from everyone else, leaning with the front of his thighs on the parapet, clutching his glass of gin and tonic in one hand and staring straight ahead. The building was on the uppermost end of East Side and before him stretched the drab depressive view of East Harlem and on the right and further north, beyond the wide and mildly cheering silver strip of the East River, that of the South Bronx.

Knowing him well she was sure he was in one of his gloomy Existentialist moods, she suspected, brought on by the gray weather, depressing landscape, and the little cemetery of decapitated crosses on top of the structure in the center. More of such cemeteries, sometimes much larger and more overcrowded, could be seen on top of the surrounding buildings as well as on some distant ones, which must have had an added effect. Life was absurd, a never-ending bout of nausea, and there was no point in living it.

Suddenly an incredible fear gripped her heart, such as she didn't remember having felt ever before—she could go up to him at that very instant, give him a push, and make him fall to his death. They were up on the fourteenth floor and he was sure not to survive it. Everybody was busy talking to others, turned the other way, and wouldn't see what she'd done. She would explain he had jumped by himself during one of his frequent known bouts of depression brought on by the weather, the depressing landscape, and the sight of the TV antenna cemeteries all around him.

She was unable to breathe, as if having been punched in the stomach. All she had to do was to walk a dozen steps and give him a push in the back. She'd been dreaming about doing such a thing practically since the day they met. Now was her chance. A few steps and a push. Her goal accomplished. A proof of who she was—Red Maureen.

Somehow she relaxed a bit and was able to catch her breath. Made a step forward. But then everything collapsed in a heap inside her. All her plans and wishes, her image of herself, were gone. She was a little girl named Greta Kraus and didn't know what to do. Tears welled up in her eyes and a gasp of crying rose up in her throat.

The sound burst out of her mouth, she turned away, made a beeline for the door, reached it, and proceeded running down the stairs. Her drink was no longer in her hand. She'd dropped it somewhere.

The apartment was on the top floor, a couple of doors away. I'd been left unlocked, so that people could come and go. She would run to the bathroom and would lock herself in.

15

———

Luckily it was empty, she turned on the light, shut the door, locked it, and quickly ran up to the mirror as if it was the toilet bowl, her bladder was full, and she couldn't wait until she relieved herself in it. She stared at her image looking back at her and as always in these situations, holding her breath, began to strain, seeing her face swell up and turn red and her eyes bulge out of her head more and more, feeling at the same time with relief the hatred inside her grow stronger and stronger.

It was doing it too slowly for her liking however, so she strained harder, making loud groaning noises in order to help herself, Uuuh, uuuh, uuuh!

Her face was growing gradually more and more puffy and redder and redder and her eyes progressively rounder and rounder and bulging more and more out of her head, but although she was making progress, she wanted to move faster and so strained ever harder, continuing to make the loud groaning sounds, not sure she'd ever stop.

Her face was now frightening—round like a big loaf of old-fashioned rye bread and red as a beet, with the eyes like white glass balls, each with two dark concentric circles in the center protruding out of it, but she continued straining and as she was doing it heard loud pounding on the door, accompanied by calls, Gretchen! Gretchen! Open up! It's me! What's wrong with you?

It was her husband.

She didn't want to interrupt what she was doing, so continued straining and groaning, and he banged on the door again and called, What's wrong with you, sweetheart? Are you alright? Why are you making these horrible sounds?

Gretchen!? He yelled after a few seconds' pause when she didn't answer.

Red Maureen, she said loudly, not tearing herself away from the mirror.

What did you say? He yelled in a desperate voice. I can't understand what you're saying.

Red Maureen, she replied raising her voice a little.

Dead marine? He yelled, even more desperate. What do you mean? You don't make any sense. And as she went on with her straining and groaning, he asked pleadingly, Why are you making these horrible sounds?

Angry now for not being left in peace, she turned to the door and yelled at the top of her voice, Why the hell can't you leave me alone? I'm constipated!

PART TWO

1

―――――

The heat hit him the moment he stepped out the door and set foot on the rickety platform at the top of the ramp stairs that'd been wheeled up against the side of the plane, like a huge bundle of bedlinen taken out of a washing machine still hot and damp, thrust into his arms for him to hold before being put in the dryer. It was bad in the summer in the Northeast but this was in a class of its own. Now he understood what it meant when people said it was hot in the tropics.

Beyond the empty white rectangle of the tarmac, barely encroached upon by the low, flat-roofed brick building of the terminal, on the far side of the bright green strip of closely-mowed grass stood a dense wall of trees—the jungle, he thought—green and tall but not as dark and as tall as he'd expected and with surprisingly spindly tree trunks running top to bottom, white and undulating like threads of nerves on the background of a sliced-through layer of flesh.

He was thinking of the jungle in real tropics—the Congo or Brazil—not realizing that where he was finding himself at the moment was not the same. The name "MERIDA" spelled out in tall red capital letters along the edge of the roof announced it for him, but he ignored the message. In his mind Mexico was in the tropics and all tropics were the same.

Inside, the big empty hall with its shiny mirror-like floor of polished light brown and white onyx was barely impacted by the handful of people that had gotten out of the plane. They huddled together as if afraid of the threatening emptiness around them. The Merida airport wasn't a busy place—at least not at the moment.

As they waited for their luggage he noticed a beautiful blonde girl dressed in a red sweatshirt, a pair of very short denim shorts, and flat thin-strapped red sandals on her feet, with sparkling sapphire eyes that sent out blue flashes like an electronic device signals in all directions and was overcome by a wave of sadness. He remembered being young and full of hope—certainty—for a bright future and wished this is what he was now. She looked to be around sixteen and he thought that if he was about her age, something might develop between them and his life would be different from what it had turned out to be.

Although not planning to take his eyes off the girl he accidentally turned his head aside and saw his wife walking toward him. She'd gone to the bathroom to take care of her bladder and the remnants of her period which had been nearly over before they left but was reawakened by the plane ride. Her midriff and hips were visibly uncomfortable in her stiff navy-blue jeans and tried to get out by bulging desperately over their sharp waistband. Her heavy breasts also tried to free themselves by spilling forward but were prevented from achieving this by the big bra clearly visible under the tight, short-sleeved mustard-colored top she wore. In contrast with the mirror-like floor, her light brown hair shone dull on her skull, pulled tight and tied in a ponytail in the back. There was a big round dark stain on the lower left side of her face—cheek and jaw—a discoloring brought on by an extended use of the contraceptive pill that looked like part of the gloom she carried inside. They were in the process of deciding on what new contraception method to switch to but hadn't reached yet a decision. She had once developed a huge knot in her hair by not combing it properly for a couple of months and finally had to cut it out with scissors. The clump was the size of a big fist and he found the way it looked unpleasant. The stain had always reminded him of it and that was one of the reasons he disliked it.   He looked at her with discomfort as she approached him.

You're still here, darling? She said on coming up to him. They haven't brought the luggage?

No, he replied sulkily. This is Mexico, not the US or Europe. I don't know what's taking them so long. We're the only plane on the tarmac. God knows how much longer we'll be here.

What with waiting for their luggage, passing through customs and passport control, and arranging for transportation, it was

Yuriy Tarnawsky

another hour before they found themselves on the bus bound
for the hotel.

2

The girl and her parents were on the bus too. It turned out they were staying at the same hotel.

The seats were arranged four across, with the aisle in the middle. He sat on the left side in the window seat, with his wife on his right and the girl in the window seat in the same row on the right, with her mother next to her. The father sat in the window seat behind them.

The bus traveled down a straight four-lane highway cutting through a perfectly flat landscape, at times industrial, with small, flat-roofed, single-storied factories or workshops, at others—empty fields overgrown with grass and scrubby shrubs interspersed with occasional palms trees, solitary or in small clusters, which seemed to want to have as little to do with the other vegetation as possible. Low, makeshift barbed-wire fences ran along the side of the road for short stretches in places. Occasionally they would pass huge trees growing on the side of the road resembling miniature mountains, with dark green foliage looking like tiny acacia leaves and big bright read blossoms like cocky roosters spoiling for a fight, sticking provocatively out of them.

He sat partly turned to the right, his left shoulder pressed against the wall of the bus, trying with little success to catch sight of the girl who most of the time leaned back in her seat with her head turned right, looking out the window, almost completely hidden by her mother. She'd taken off the sweatshirt and had put it away somewhere and had on what looked like an embroidered white-on-white Mexican shirt she must have worn underneath. Only when she stirred occasionally and sat up or leaned forward was he able to refresh in his memory her profile, delicate as a watermark in a sheet of expensive paper. Sometimes she would also turn toward her mother and stay that way for a few seconds talking to her and then he was able to reconstitute in his mind the image of her full face.

He was angry with the situation and fidgeted constantly as if physically uncomfortable in his seat, at times leaning way forward and craning his neck to the right so as to better see the girl, but tried to restrain himself so as not to appear too brazen. There was no plan in his action rather than simply his wanting to see the girl. He was like a drug addict hopelessly hooked on the beauty of her face.

As was customary with her on such occasions his wife started up a conversation with the girl's mother and from it he learned that the latter was called Pearl, the girl—Sapphire, and the father—Simon, their last name was Koenig, they were Canadian, lived in London, Ontario, where the father was professor of Spanish and Hispanic studies at the university, they loved Mexico, had been visiting it for years, had been to Merida when their daughter was little, and had come down this time to let her see the city and the archeological sites around it so that she would appreciated them now that she was older. They planned to spend some time in the city, to enjoy its attractions, but also to visit the archeological sites of Uxmal and Chichen Itza, the first one the day after tomorrow and the second one the day after that.

They reached the city, drove first down a straight broad avenue with shady tress on both sides and a divider with flowers and shrubs in the middle, then through straight narrow streets with no trace of vegetation in them, lined with single- or two-storied stone or stucco houses, the latter painted various bright colors—yellow, ocher, red, purple, blue, green, rarely white—flush against each other, bars on their windows, their doors shut, fancy ancient-looking carvings above many of the latter, and finally stopped at the side entrance of the hotel where all the passengers got out, filed into the lobby, and queued up at the registration desk while their luggage was brought in. The hotel stood on the corner of two streets, the main—clearly older—part of it two-storied, and a tall, perhaps ten stories high modern-looking addition in the back.

There was a big square open patio in the middle of the main part with graceful arches supported by slender columns running along it on both floors, and the registration desk was on the first floor along one of the walls under the arches.

While standing in line, waiting for their turn to register, watching the hotel workers bring in and arrange the luggage and people milling around it, he couldn't keep his eyes off the girl and at one point observed how organically her thighs emerged from under the short, tight-fitting jeans like sprouts coming out of a germinating seed, feeling for the first time sexual desire for her stir itself inside him. He imagined what it was like in the spot where her thighs met under the clothes and began seeing some vague scenes with it and him in them curling and uncurling like clouds in his mind, but when he found himself facing the clerk at the other side of the registration desk he put an abrupt end to that and devoted himself to the task at hand.

When they had finished registering and were picking out their luggage to be taken up to their room he saw the girl and her parents go up the few steps leading to where the elevators were located, turn right, and disappear behind the corner of the wall, and pushed the thoughts about her fully out of his mind so that it seemed he'd never had them. They'd been nothing more than silly fantasizing. The girl was gone and he would most likely never see her again.

3

Exhausted from the trip, after a simple meal of tacos and beer at a little restaurant in the nearby Plaza Grande—main square—they returned to the hotel and went to bed.

That night he had the following dream.

He is facing his wife while they are both standing on top of a tightly stretched cable high above ground in a vast dark space that seems to be an empty cathedral. He feels unsteady on his feet and is relying on her holding his hands which he keeps stretched out before him. She is doing fine however—she looks steady and is smiling while staring into his eyes.

But suddenly she lets go of his hands and starts backing away, still smiling but now motioning with her hands for him to back away too. It seems to be some kind of a game they are playing. They've been standing together on a tightly stretched rope high above the ground in the middle of an empty space and now are supposed to back away from each other to where the rope is attached on their side.

He is terrified by what is happening and feels certain he won't be able to make it to his spot. He is sure he'll fall sooner or later.

He has no choice however and will try to make it there. Attempting to balance himself with his arms he carefully puts one of his feet behind him, shifts the weight of his body accordingly, and plans to move his other foot back.

The cable underneath him sways as he does that and he notices it isn't as tight as it seemed before. It sags and feels soft.

He looks at it and sees that it isn't a metal cable as he'd thought but something wider, uneven, and white. It looks like one of those roots of trees coming down from the ceiling in the picture of the cenote the Kaufmanns had shown them. He realizes also that they are not in a cathedral but in a cave over an underground well like the one in the picture—apparently that very same one.

The realization terrifies him because he knows it'll be even harder for him to make it to the other side than he thought. But still he tries to keep his balance and moves his other foot back.

He focuses on the image of his wife and sees that she has moved quite a distance away from him and keeps smiling and motioning with her hands for him to move back while she herself is backing off.

He sways more from side to side however, tries to keep his balance, and in despair glances over his shoulder and sees something white and thin coming down from above like a girl's naked arm reaching out to him, trying to help him.

Overjoyed, he reaches out for it with his hand, grabs it, but it is too thin and slippery for him to hold on to and slips out of his fingers. He loses his balance and starts falling into the emptiness below. He realizes then it wasn't a hand at all that he had tried to grab but something long and slippery—undoubtedly another one of those tree roots coming down from the ceiling, and concludes with sadness that even if he'd managed to hold onto it, it wouldn't have helped him since he wouldn't have been able to hold onto it for long.

As he falls he raises his eyes and sees his wife standing high above him, steady, as if on solid ground, a wide ear to ear grin on her face.

4

___

He woke up at the break of dawn and couldn't go back to sleep, so decided to go for a dip in the hotel swimming pool in the patio down below. He was sure there wouldn't be anyone there at such an early hour and he would be able to relax all alone on one of the lounge chairs and enjoy the fresh morning air and the cool water. It'd been unbearably hot the day before and he expected it to be much more comfortable then.

His wife was sound asleep in the other bed facing away from him, rolled up into a messy ball in the bedclothes, still as a mummy, and the room felt hostile, the furniture like a bunch of huge bulging sharp-cornered eyes staring menacingly at him—the massive beds, white like all the furniture in the room, the matching squat bedside table between them with the big white lamp on it, the round table in the middle of the room and the four matching chairs around it, the dresser against the wall on the left and the likewise white-framed mirror on the dark green wall above it, the contents of the room reflected in it looking like smashed-up furniture piled up in a niche in the wall, sticking haphazardly out of it.

The patio was empty of people when he got there and at first he thought his wish had come true but then he noticed a towel lying in a messy heap on one of the chairs with a pair of black rubber thongs under it and after that a solitary figure doing laps in the pool, leaving transient stains of white light around itself on the pale blue surface of the water.

It was a woman in a black one-piece swimming suit and a light blue rubber cap on her head, and for an instant the thought crossed his mind how wonderful it would be if the woman turned out to be the girl. But he dismissed it before it bloomed into something bigger—such things happened in novels and not in real life, and if they did happen in real life it was with people who were lucky. He had always considered himself not to be one of them.

He was wearing his swimming trunks under the robe and was planning to go in the water but felt reluctant to do it as yet— the pool was small, he didn't want to be in the way of the woman swimmer, and at any rate he still wasn't ready to get wet. He had to get in the right mood for it.

The pool being small, there were only a few lounge chairs around it and he put his towel on the farthest one away from the one with the woman's things, stepped out of his thongs, left them on the ground next to the chair, and stretched out on it in his robe. The air was humid but felt cool, and sunshine wasn't penetrating onto the patio.

The latter was framed by the walls of the hotel and the neighboring building on three sides, with the fourth one shielded from the street by a high stucco wall. It was overgrown with a climbing plant with shiny dark green leaves and bloomed with beautiful bright red flowers. He lay facing it, relaxing, closing and opening his eyes, not thinking about anything, refreshing his inner peace with the sight of the green wall and the red flowers before him.

He'd nearly drifted off into sleep when he heard the sound of loud splashing coming from the pool. Coming back to life he turned his face in that direction and saw the woman had finished swimming and was climbing out of the water.

She walked gingerly to her chair, picked up the towel, and proceeded to dry herself off with it. After a while she removed her cap, letting her hair fall out of it like a big splash of white water, and went on drying herself, pushing the hair aside as she rubbed the skin under it.

Reminded vaguely of something although not sure of what, unable to arrange his thoughts into a coherent pattern in spite of trying hard, he followed the woman's movements with his eyes and as she turned her face toward him, looked in his eyes, and smiled a broad white smile, he realized it was the girl. The shower of sapphire-blue sparks being shot in his direction couldn't have been emitted by anyone else's eyes but hers. It was her he'd been reminded of. She looked much more mature in the swimming suit than in the street clothes and he wouldn't admit the possibility it could be her.

Still smiling and continuing to dry herself she came over to him, sat down on the neighboring chair, and said in a cheerful voice, You're Walter, right?

Yes, he said, his heart giving a wild leap as he sat up. She had referred to him by his first name!

You're a philosopher... teach philosophy at a college, she went on. My father has read your book. It's about Exit... Extis...?

Existentialism, he interrupted her gently, turning toward her and putting his feet on the ground while smiling a broad smile, all bright inside. Yes.

Exis... Existentialism? She said. What is Existentialism? She stopped drying herself and draped the towel over the top of her thighs.

Oh, he said, it's a long story, but it can be described as a school of thought that maintains that man is responsible for everything he does and answers only to himself and not to others. Whether he is happy or not depends solely on him and he can be grateful to or blame only himself for it.

That's interesting, she said. I'd like to learn more about it.

You should take a course on it when you're in college, he said jokingly. Why don't you come to our school when you're ready and take one with me.

Perhaps I will, she replied, laughing. I've been toying with the idea of going to university in the US. It's more interesting than Canada, she added, getting up from the chair, holding the towel in her hand.

You're going already? He asked in an anxious voice.

Yes, she said, I've been here a long time. It's getting late. I have to take a shower before we go down to breakfast and then we're going sightseeing. There's a lot to see in the city.

Tomorrow we're going to Uxmal and the day afterwards to Chichen Itza, she went on. Are you going too? She asked, starting to move away from him in the direction of her chair.

I don't know about Uxmal, he replied, getting up himself, but Chichen Itza for sure. We're going to visit a cenote nearby there, so will definitely visit the site.

Great, she said, starting to turn around. Maybe we'll see each other there. Good-bye.

Yes... good-bye, he said barely audibly as she turned away and watched her go up to her chair, step into her thongs, pick up her cap, and walk toward the door leading into the building.

About half-way to it she turned around, smiled, lifted her arm, made a little frilly gesture with her fingers in his direction, and said once more, Good-bye.

Speechless, as if confused, he waved back at her and saw her turn away, walk to the door, and disappear in the darkness behind it.

5

―――

After breakfast, armed with the map of the city and instructions how to get there, which they got at the hotel from the attendant at the registration desk, they set out to Mercado Lucas De Gálvez, the market where the Kaufmanns had found the driver that drove them to the cenote, hoping to find him themselves. His wife had carefully written down the name of the place on a piece of paper together with that of the driver and the cenote and had guarded it carefully as the apple of her eye.

He hadn't been very keen on going to the cenote and agreed to the idea because of seeing how much his wife wanted to do it, but after the conversation with the girl at the pool that morning had regrets about it. He felt he'd much rather forget about the place and go on a regular excursion tour together with the girl and her parents, not only to Chichen Itza moreover, but also to Uxmal, since this would give him more chance to see her. He and his wife had vaguely agreed to see the former site but made no firm plans about it. As they walked he hoped they wouldn't find the driver and would do what he himself wanted instead.

The morning was cool, much more comfortable than the night before, and they walked slowly next to each other in the direction they were told, looking around, he occasionally stepping aside to let someone pass in either direction on the narrow sidewalks.

Going past the huge San Idelfonso cathedral in the main square he expressed a desire to step inside and have a look at it, which they did, but stayed there only a couple of minutes, remaining by the door, his wife insisting they move on so as to find the driver, as if they'd made arrangements to meet him at a certain time and would miss him if they were late. She was utterly possessed by the idea but that didn't surprise him since she would often act like this over something before unexpectedly dropping it and showing no interest in it whatever.

The remnants of his Catholic upbringing stirring deep inside him, he found the vast Piranesian interior of the church with its shiny wooden benches stretching from the entrance all the way to the altar, a huge figure of Christ on the cross behind it, intriguing, and wanted to stay on for a while, but anxious to move on, she showed no interest in it in spite of having planned to be a nun—join the order of Poor Clares—at one time. She was born a protestant but converted to Catholicism while still in High School and had shown at the beginning the fervor typical of a neophyte.

In spite of following the map and instructions, they got lost a few times but finally arrived at the market. At first they thought they'd come to the wrong place even though the sign above the entrance clearly announced it was the one they were looking for. Based on the pictures of the interior the Kaufmanns had showed them they thought it was devoted exclusively to local arts and crafts, whereas from the side they entered, it appeared to deal in produce and other sort of food as well as household things, children's toys, and clothes. Eventually however they did arrive at the arts and crafts section which was on the other side of the building and, as they'd been told, next to it, alongside a columned porch, the open space where people were picked up and dropped off and where taxicabs were stationed.

When they asked for a driver named Nicanor nobody stepped up at first however, and when, after some calling around by some of the drivers, one did, he clearly wasn't the right one, being fair-looking, with European features and light brown hair. Nobody knew of another Nicanor driver who wasn't there either.

As to inquiries about a cenote called Pozo del Diablo near Chichen Itza—they produced in response nothing but shaking of heads and shrugging of shoulders and suggestions to go to Chichen Itza and look for a driver there, and so, after only a few minutes' time they were forced to admit their quest to find the driver had come to naught. To get to the cenote they had to try something else.

His wife was visibly disappointed—silent and gloomy-faced, but he was overjoyed. Maybe they would go to Uxmal and Chichen Itza on an excursion tour and he would get to see the girl after all. He didn't want to show his feelings however and tried to look disappointed too, consoling his wife that the taxi drivers were right—they should take an excursion tour to Chichen Itza and look for someone there. He'd always thought looking for that particular driver was like searching for a needle in a haystack and that they should have planned to go to Chichen Itza from the beginning.

It was lunchtime already and there were all sorts of interesting-looking restaurants at the market but they decided to eat at the hotel instead, as if punishing the place for not having let them find the driver there.

By then it had gotten uncomfortably warm and when they had crawled back to the hotel, unexpectedly, they ran in the lobby into the Koenigs—husband and wife alone. The girl wasn't with them.

When they explained to the people what'd happened, they were told they shouldn't worry. They should indeed take an excursion tour to Chichen Itza and would surely find a taxi driver there who could take them to the well. The local people were bound to know about it. They could skip part of the tour or go there during the lunch hour or later and have the driver take them back to Merida. They themselves were going there the day after tomorrow and perhaps they would like to join them. Tomorrow they were going to Uxmal. Weren't they planning to go there? Perhaps they could join them on that excursion too. The tour office was open and they could go there together right now and check.

He found the proposal a dream come true, his wife had no objections, and so the four of them went to the office, it turned out that the tours weren't filled, they booked their seats, and agreed to meet the people that night at eight in the lobby to go together to dinner at a Spanish restaurant the latter knew. They had been to it before, found the food there delicious, and the place had good music to boot.

6

_____

When they came down to the lobby in the evening, he was stunned. There were the Koenigs waiting for them once again alone. The girl wasn't coming. She'd met some Americans, boys and girls of the same age as she when they were sightseeing that day and went out with them for a night on the town. He was overjoyed when her parents had suggested they have dinner together, imagining sitting across the table from her and spending the whole evening feasting on her face, and now had learned that that was not to be. The sky had fallen and what was he to do?

But after a minute or two he began to feel better. They were going together to Uxmal the next day and to Chichen Itza the following one, so he would see her essentially two full days in a row. That was nothing to complain about. Besides he was going to spend the evening in her parents' company, which was a little like spending time with her, and in addition the place they were going to sounded interesting. He cheered up and decided to have a good time.

The restaurant was a few blocks away from the hotel and they went there on foot. It was called Mesón Castellano—Castilian Inn—and was located in what seemed to have been once a private home. It consisted of four or five rooms, none of them big, with about half a dozen tables in each. The doors between the rooms had been removed, so waiters and guests were able to move freely between them.

The rooms were painted different colors, the one they sat in a delicate matte green. The door and window frames were a shiny black, which contrasted effectively with the color and texture of the walls. Dark red, almost maroon tablecloths covered the tables.

They drank sangria served in a big round glass pitcher, had grilled chorizo and prawns for appetizers, and for dinner, all of them, gazpacho, grilled steak with sage served on round wooden pallets with a grove around the edge to catch the juice, and coconut-flavored flan. The steak knives provided had plain wooden handles and triangular blades like those you see in paintings by old masters, for instance Breughel. They were sharp and worked very well. The Koenigs had settled on the choices first and as they said these were good, he and his wife decided to order the same.

There was a singer who accompanied himself on the guitar who went from room to room singing a few songs in each. He looked young—in his twenties—had blond, sand-colored hair, and was dressed in regular street clothes—a white shirt with a grid of thin black stripes and gray pants.

About in the middle of their meal he came into their room, sat down on a chair that stood there in the corner, put his left foot on a little stool he had brought along, tuned the guitar a little, looked down, touched the strings, threw his head back, and staring into the open proceeded singing and playing.

From the very first sounds he heard he knew he was going to be profoundly affected by the song. It was as if he sensed that the frequencies of its notes, the physical vibrations, would open some sealed chambers in his soul, letting emotions hidden in them come out into the open. He didn't know what these were but sensed they involved great joy as well as pain and had something to do with the girl.

The song went on and, yes, the feelings were about her—the immense joy of loving her and the excruciating pain at her not being there.

The song was in Spanish and curious about it, he leaned over to the girl's father and asked what it was about and if it was Mexican. The latter whispered discretely that it was Spanish and not Mexican, from the region of Andalusia, and was called "Camino Verde," meaning "Green Road."

Seeing how interested he was in the song, the man proceeded translating it for him as it was being sung, and the two sat

Yuriy Tarnawsky

leaning toward each other, he with his ear toward the latter, and the latter with his lips close to his ear.

The song went as follows:

Hoy he vuelto a pasar
Por aquel camino verde
Que por el valle se pierde
Dejando mi soledad.

Por el camino verde, camino verde que va a la ermita
Desde que tú te fuiste lloran de pena las margaritas.
La fuente se ha secado y las azucenas están marchitas
Por el camino verde, camino verde que va a la ermita.

Hoy he vuelto a rezar
En la sombra de la ermita
Y a pedir a la virgencita
Que vuelva mi felicidad.

Por el camino verde, camino verde que va a la ermita
Desde que tú te fuiste lloran de pena las margaritas.
La fuente se ha secado y las azucenas están marchitas
Por el camino verde, camino verde que va a la ermita.

Which means:

Today I have returned to walk
Along that green road

Which disappears in the valley
Leaving behind my solitude.

Along the green road, the green road that leads to the
       hermitage
Since you went away daisies cry out of anguish.
The fountain has run dry and the lilies have wilted
Along the green road, the green road that leads to the
       hermitage.

Today I have returned to pray
In the shadow of the hermitage
And to beg the little Virgin
For my happiness to come back.

Along the green road, the green road that leads to the
       hermitage
Since you went away daisies cry out of anguish.
The fountain has run dry and the lilies have wilted
Along the green road, the green road that leads to the
       hermitage.

He wasn't able to catch all the words the man was saying, but those that stuck in his memory were "Walk, green road, hermitage, disappears, solitude, since you went away daisies cry out of anguish, fountain, dry, lilies, wilted, pray, little Virgin, happiness, come back."

The song ended, and the man went on to sing other songs but he continued sitting mesmerized as if hearing the first one being sung over and over, his food and drink untouched.

After singing another three or four songs the man stopped and it looked as though he was going to move to another room.

A wild idea then shot up in his head—he would go up to the man and ask him to sing the song again. He had never done anything like that before and under normal circumstances would have mulled over it for a long time before acting, but this time instantly got up, went over to the man, and bending down, asked him to be so kind as to sing the first song again. He liked it immensely. Mechanically, he stuck his hand in his pants pocket, pulled out a few bills he found there, and offered them to the man.

The latter shook his head, refusing the offer, nodded in agreement, and started getting ready to sing.

He thanked the man, put the money back in his pocket, turned around, and proud inside, as if taller, went back to their table, seeing the Koenigs look at him with approving smiles on their faces and his wife with a stare that seemed a mixture of amazement and disapproval.

The singing started before he had reached his chair and he heard applause explode all over the room. It looked as though everyone had fallen in love with the song, the same as he.

As he walked he saw that the Koenigs were applauding but he wasn't sure of his wife.

7

_____

When they were walking back to the hotel, still under the spell of the song, he didn't take part in the conversation going on between the Koenigs and his wife but continued thinking about the former, and as he recalled the phrase "daisies cry out of anguish," which he had found most moving, he observed that in his case the daisies in addition to crying would be grinding their teeth.

Later that night he had the following dream.

He and his wife are at a restaurant, having a meal.

They're alone in an empty room with bare white walls and tall curtainless windows with dirty glass panes, so that you can't see through them outside.

They're sitting behind a plain square wooden table facing each other, with small aluminum buckets in front of each of them. The buckets are full of boiled bones, they each pick out a bone, chew the meat and gristle off it, throw it into a bigger aluminum bucket that sits on the side on the table, pick out another bone, chew on it, and repeat the whole process.

The bones appear to have been freshly boiled, are warm, there's plenty of stuff on them to chew, it tastes good, and he's pleased with the choice of the restaurant they've made. He's glad they came there.

He usually concentrates on the bone he's chewing on, keeping his eyes on it, so as to make sure he's chewing everything off it before throwing it away.

It's been quiet in the room so far, with only the smacking of lips, swallowing, and so forth of each of them disturbing the silence. But suddenly he hears a harsh grating noise coming from in front of him, sounding like bone grinding on bone.

He stops eating, lifts his eyes, and sees it's his wife chewing on a big bone which she has laid down on the table, is holding it down with both hands, and is gnawing on it with the teeth on one side of her mouth like a dog trying to crack a bone. She's chewing on the bone where there's nothing to eat, so it indeed looks like she's trying to crack it.

He finds it amazing, lowers his hand with the bone he's been chewing on himself so as to see better, and looks at her carefully.

Yuriy Tarnawsky

The bone is big, looking like part of a femur belonging to a big man, and she's definitely set at cracking it—she has opened her mouth real wide so that her molars are gripping the bone, and is biting down with them on the bone as hard as she can. They keep sliding off however, making an unpleasant grinding noise, but she doesn't give up, bites down again, and keeps on trying. She looks like she's completely lost her senses—her eyes are popping out of her head and you can tell she's not looking with them, saliva is flowing out of her mouth, having formed a puddle on the table, and she's making loud growling sounds as if pretending to be a dog.

She's biting down on the bone harder and harder, making progressively louder and louder grinding sounds as well as growling louder and louder, and in the end he can't stand it any longer and yells at the top of his voice, For god's sake, Greta, stop! Greta stop!

He then woke up.

His wife had a tendency to gnash her teeth in her sleep, which he found annoying, and for a moment he thought that that's what she'd been doing, causing him to have the dream. The room was dead still however.

He turned his head right and looked toward the other bed, where she slept. She lay rolled up into a ball on her side, turned away from him.

8

It was a glorious morning in every way possible. The air was cooler and fresher again than the night before, they had a nice breakfast at the hotel, he saw the girl and her parents across a couple of tables, they all exchanged silent and verbal greetings, filed into the bus together, and were driving down to Uxmal.

He sat in the aisle seat with his wife on the left, the girl with her mother were in the seats before them, the former directly in front of him, and the father across the aisle from her. He could see the top of her head above the backrest of the seat and it was as good as if she were next to him. They were together.

The bus drove down a perfectly straight highway cutting through a flat landscape consisting largely of plantations of unruly henequen plants, their sword-like leaves menacingly sticking in a helter-skelter fashion out of the ground. Occasionally one of them had a tall thin stalk rising into the air in the center, looking like a stake driven into it to kill it as would have been done with a warlock or a witch in some countries in the old days. These plants were invariably withered and smaller than the other ones and it really looked as if they were dead.

Banks of green trees loomed tall on the horizon.

From time to time they passed through little villages—hamlets—of perhaps a dozen huts with walls made out of thin uneven sticks driven into the ground in the form of a rectangle with rounded corners, capped with a thick thatched roof, with no windows and a plain opening for a door, occasionally displaying a lone sagging hammock seemingly floating in the air inside. The interiors looked dark but they were probably reasonably light because of the daylight penetrating through the gaps between the sticks forming the walls. Air undoubtedly could also pass freely through the gaps and he observed that this was probably the reason uneven sticks were used for the walls in order to keep the huts cooler in the hot climate.

Women dressed in loose short-sleeved calf-long dresses made out of white cloth, embroidered along necks, edges of sleeves, and hems, could be sometimes seen doing chores in the yard such as sweeping the ground with what looked like a thin bundle of reeds, carrying pots, and so forth, or simply standing up, watching the bus drive by.

In one such hamlet the driver pulled into a little open area at the side of the road, stopped, got out without turning off the engine or saying anything, and quickly ran to a hut somewhat bigger than most they had passed, which stood in the shadow of a few tall trees and had a sign "CANTINA" in big black capital letters clumsily painted on a rectangular white shield sticking up on the roof. The tour guide, a woman who'd welcomed them on the bus and had spoken a little through a microphone about where they were going and what they would see as the bus first started moving, said nothing about it, and it looked as though the driver had done it on his own on the spur of the moment, without consulting with her, deciding to pick up something he needed. When he emerged out of the store a minute or two later he was indeed clutching something small in his hand which looked like a pack of cigarettes. He didn't light one up however, so he must have gotten it for later, knowing he was out of them.

A bunch of small palm trees ten to fifteen feet tall clustered in one corner of the yard in front of the building and as they waited for the driver to come back he watched a brood of piglets, about half a dozen of them, led by their mother, running around playfully in the shadow of the palm trees. They were small, much smaller and darker-skinned than the pigs you normally see in America, with long thin bodies overgrown with sparse red hair, likewise long snouts, and tall legs. There was a little mound of earth under one of the palms and the piglets all tried to stand on top of it but as soon as one managed to do it, one of the other ones would push it off, take its place, and the process would be repeated. During all of this the mother went on about her business sniffing and digging with her snout as if not caring what her charges were doing but you could tell she was following them closely with her beady black little eyes. This went on and on with no sign of stopping and there was no trace of evil in the piglets' behavior except pure, innocent fun.

A little farther along, as they were approaching another hamlet, two huge black buzzards with long, curving beaks and hideous bare necks that looked like penises swollen with blood sat on a tree, keeping their eyes on the road, watching out for anything that might be of interest to them.

Finally a compound of modern-looking buildings appeared on the left side of the road and as the bus drove on he saw through the sleazy thicket of trees on the right confusing images of ill-defined, crumbling shapes like frames of a film cast onto a screen by a malfunctioning projector, and then a huge structure of white stone appeared above the tops of the trees like a gigantic elephant laboriously trying to get up on its feet, which he recognized as the Pyramid of the Magician which he had read about in the brochure he'd picked up at the hotel. Just then the woman guide began speaking through the microphone, letting everyone know they had arrived in Uxmal and would be getting off the bus momentarily.

The latter drove on a little longer, slowed down, pulled into a parking area where there were other busses standing with people milling around them, came to a stop, and everyone began filing out.

As he got out himself he stopped as if unable to move, having his breath knocked out by the incredible sight before him.

Rather than resembling an elephant the pyramid looked like an enormous cone-shaped mound of white stone piled up by a gigantic excavator. It wasn't square like Egyptian pyramids but broad and narrow, with rounded corners, not unlike those in the huts they saw coming down on the bus, and had four levels, each higher one somewhat smaller than the one below it, with open platforms on the tops of the first three levels running around the bases of the ones above. The first two levels had steep inclined sides of small shiny stone encased in mortar. The other two had vertical walls of smooth hewn stone. The fourth level consisted of a structure that looked like a temple which had an ill-defined, as it appeared partly crumbling decoration on top. A wide and very steep staircase ran up the middle of the broader side of the first level from the ground to its top, with a heavy iron chain laid out along it for people to hold on to as they went up or down. Judging by what those on the staircase were doing, it was more useful for coming down than for going up. Smaller staircases provided access to the next three levels.

They were shown first the great pyramid, then the so-called Nunnery, the Governor's palace, the House of the Turtles, and the Ball Court, and finally were permitted to explore the site on their own.

As he was doing this, while standing on the platform on the third level of the pyramid, the edge of its vertical side a short step before him, drinking in with his eyes the vast, breath-taking vista in front he realized to his great satisfaction he was a different man than he had been just an hour or two earlier.

He felt it was partly due to his feeling about himself and the girl. The sensation of them being together he had first experienced on the bus was extended and even deepened in the course of the tour. They didn't talk much to each other or spend any time alone but did exchange glances, nods, and an occasional word or two as they passed each other in the crowd while moving from one structure to another or while exploring a particular one. To him the relationship between them felt solid, as if they'd been together for a long time and would stay this way forever from then on.

Another reason though, and he felt the more important one, was the fact that the art and architecture he had been exploring was built on esthetic principles diametrically opposed to those he had been brought up on. Western esthetics valued slenderness and graceful proportions, principles inherited from the ancient Greeks, whereas the structures and carvings here were stocky and often top-heavy, but beautiful in their own way nonetheless. Since this was true, he could chuck all the rules and regulations he'd been sticking to so religiously until then and follow new ones he made up himself. He didn't have to stay married to his wife, didn't have to consider how the Koenigs felt if he and their daughter were to fall in love, and didn't have to worry what other people thought about the age difference between him and the girl. It was for them to decide how to live. The problem with her being underage would somehow be resolved.

As to her, he realized she wasn't with him at the moment but decided it didn't matter. She was somewhere nearby, probably on the same level on the other side, and they would see each other in a few minutes. Although momentarily apart, they were together.

He looked at his feet and saw they were not much more than a foot away from the edge of the platform, with the wall below it going vertically down to the next level. It wasn't that far down to it but if he were to fall down to that level, bounce off it, fall down to the next one and to the next one after that all the way to the ground, he hated to think what would be left of him. Chills ran up his spine as he considered the prospect.

Without knowing why, he quickly turned his head right and saw his wife a few feet away, looking at him in a strange way.

Instinctively he stepped back and turned his head forward. Did she guess what changes had taken place in him? He wondered.

He pushed the thought immediately out of his mind however. He didn't care if she did.

Yuriy Tarnawsky

The green canopy of tree tops stretched unbroken in all directions all the way to the horizon. He was flying by himself high up in the sky above it.

9

They all had lunch at the restaurant in the hotel which was part of the compound on the left side of the road they had passed earlier that morning, under the trees and at the side of a swimming pool. After the meal the excursion was to continue to Kabah, which was as small archeological site a few miles down the road to the town of Campeche, but people were given a choice to stay at the hotel and relax at the pool if they so desired.

They had been told this back in Merida and he took his swimming trunks along in case he chose to do it but had planned to continue with the excursion together with his wife. She wasn't very fond of water and didn't bring her swimming suit along. Seeing that the girl had chosen to stay and go swimming, he decided to change his mind. He would do the same. If it appeared too obvious why he was staying and it upset his wife or the girl's parents, he didn't care. At one time he would have been too cowardly to do something so bold but he was a different person now and what other people thought didn't concern him.

He told his wife he was feeling too hot and tired and would stay and cool off in the pool and she accepted his decision without any objection. The Koenigs likewise didn't show any reaction to what he was doing. He felt relieved. This was a proof it was better to think of yourself first and not to worry about other people. Often they wouldn't even care what you did.

The bus drove off and he and the girl went to change in the separate male and female parts of the bathhouse without talking to each other. They hadn't exchanged a word since lunchtime. None of the other people who stayed behind were around. It looked like they had other plans in mind.

When he came out she wasn't there and he made himself comfortable on one of the lounge chairs by the pool in the shade of a tree so as not to be hot, waiting for her to return. He was the only one there.

A tall and thick, neatly trimmed hedge of some bushy plant with dark green waxy leaves grew on his right and as he looked at it he noticed there were a couple of iguanas hiding under it from the sun on the ground. They were perfectly still, showing no sign of life, as if dead, but he was sure they were alive and this was merely their normal way of behaving—by remaining motionless they preserved energy and didn't have to hunt for insects so much. They had been all over the ruins at the site and he saw them behaving like this—staying dead still for a while and then unexpectedly scampering off busily on some unknown errand, oblivious of people around them, as if the latter were of no importance, they being the owners and masters of the place. He had observed then that when they moved they did it very laboriously, like a bunch of pieces of greenish-gray meat clumsily tied together, threatening to come apart.

Suddenly he noticed there was a strangely shaped, large, greenish object right next to him on the ground on his right and almost jerked up in fear, ready to flee or fight, but then realized it was a big iguana, and relaxed. It was much bigger than the other two, most likely a male, the other two being probably its female mates. It had apparently been there all the time but he merely didn't notice it. It was still like the ones under the hedge and was looking at him with its round unblinking eye—only its left side was turned toward him—apparently waiting for a handout. A big frilly dewlap hung down under its chin and blood could be seen pulsing in its neck closer to its chest, the skin rising and falling in one spot at a rate of about once every two seconds.

He found the image hideous and in anger tried to shoo the creature away by yelling at it and waving his hand. It paid no attention to him however until he threatened it with his foot, when it did finally run off, moving slowly, clumsily throwing its ungainly body from side to side.

He moved his head left toward the pool and as he did that realized the dewlap on the iguana and for some reason the vein pulsing in its neck had reminded him of his wife—the dark spot on the lower half side of her face. A slight gust of wind blew by just at that instant, rippling the surface of the water like fine silk, making him feel as if it were chills running up his spine.

Once again upset, he moved his head straight, lay back in the chair, and closed his eyes, hoping to relax for a while.

But at that instant he heard a loud splash coming from the pool and as he looked there, saw a female body in a black swimming suit and a light blue rubber cap move effortlessly under the water toward the other side of the pool.

The girl was finally there.

10

Normally he would have waited to go in the water, debating how to proceed, but this time got up instantly and dove in himself, creating a tsunami that was too big for the small pool. The water on the other side from where he jumped in splashed out onto the concrete apron and for a while tried to find its proper place in the pool, thrashing about inside it, before finding a suitable position.

There was a burst of genuine laughter directed at his face when he came up and a pair of huge sapphires surrounded by a field of scattered sparkling diamonds a couple of feet away facing him, and he responded with his own burst of laughter no less genuine, they raced each other a number of times from one end of the pool to the other, she winning each time by an ever increasing length, and so he finally gave up and they sat next to each other on the edge of the pool, he badly out of breath, she hardly breathing, swinging their legs in the water and chatting.

She was on her High School swimming team, apparently a star member, planned to swim in college, hoped one day to make it to the Olympics and to make swimming her carrier. As to her age, she was still fifteen but would turn sixteen in a couple of months, in the fall.

Jumping in, she explained and then demonstrated, you should contact the water with the smallest possible surface area of your body, be as straight and as streamlined as you can so as to minimize the resistance it would offer and so that you would lose the least amount of the kinetic energy you've generated by your jump and travel faster.

He watched her demonstration, tried himself, was getting progressively better, decided to switch over to swimming, and worked on the technique of the crawl.

In the crawl you don't kick with your feet in rhythm with your arms but move them independently, rapidly, creating a stream of water moving in the opposite direction that propels you like that generated by the propeller in an outboard engine on a boat or the turbine in a jet plane.

She showed him how to do it by hanging on to the edge of the pool and moving her legs, he tried it himself, found it much harder than diving, and finally gave up. He understood how it was to be done and would practice it on his own. Right now he was too tired.

They stretched out on two adjoining lounge chairs and he decided to have a drink—a margarita for himself, he concluded.

She turned her face to him and he was overwhelmed by the proximity of her eyes. Jeepers Creepers, where did you get those peepers? He was going to say but thought it was better not to. Regardless of whether she knew where the phrase came from or not, it was bound to bring out into the open the uncomfortable difference in their age, and so he merely said, What would she like to drink? Some juice?

A piña colada, she replied.

With no alcohol?

Yes, with alcohol, she laughed. A piña colada without alcohol is not a piña colada.

But she was too young, underage.

So what, she said, they were in Mexico.

They didn't have age restrictions in Mexico?

They probably did, but they never objected. Not with foreigners at least. They are always bigger and besides Mexicans couldn't tell if you were underage or overage. They didn't know how whites aged.

But what about her parents? Wouldn't they object?

Oh, she laughed. Maybe they would, or maybe they wouldn't. With him, they probably wouldn't. But they wouldn't know, right? So why did it matter?

Yes, they wouldn't know, he thought, but he still felt uncomfortable feeding an underage girl alcohol. What if they did find out? How would they react? He didn't want to offend them. He liked them.

To hell with her parents and offending other people, he suddenly though. He was a different man now, right? So why should he care?

OK, he finally said. Piña colada with alcohol it will be. But light... light on alcohol.

Not too light, she laughed.

He didn't respond but got up and walked over to the bar which was farther away from the pool in a big *palapa* under a heavy thatched roof.

He was going to tell the barman to be light on alcohol with the piña colada but at the last moment changed his mind. Let her have it full strength. She apparently drank alcohol all the time and her parents let her do it, and besides he was a new man now, wasn't he?

He ordered the two drinks, went back, and waited for them to come, stretched out on the chair next to the girl, the two of them chatting. For a moment he thought of talking to her about Existentialism since she'd expressed interest in it at the pool in Merida but decided not to. Her professed interest was undoubtedly at least partly result of politeness and besides that was not a topic for them to discuss at the moment. If nothing else, it would once again bring into the open the uncomfortable difference in their age.

When the drinks came they clinked together their plastic cups and proceeded to sip from them and chat.

As they were doing it he noticed he was gulping his drink down fast, hoping the girl would do the same with hers, so that she would be done with it before her parents returned. He had an uncomfortable feeling the bus bringing them back would be showing up any moment. Angry with himself at still worrying about what other people thought in spite of all his professions to the contrary, he bit his teeth together and testily put his drink away on the ground next to the chair, hoping this time this would induce the girl to drink slower. As soon as she was done with this drink, he decided, he would buy her another one. It was not easy to be yourself!

11

Back in Merida, as he and his wife were going back to the hotel after having dinner at an open-air restaurant in the main square, they got caught in a veritable deluge of a downpour and were drenched literally to the skin as they arrived, cold and out of breath from running, at the hotel door.

They went straight to their room, took their showers, she first, he second, hung up their wet clothes in the bathroom after wringing them out, and went to bed. They were dead tired from the trip, it was close to ten at night, and they had to get up early in the morning to go to Chichen Itza.

It was still pouring nonstop, with the rain sounding like a waterfall outside the windows, accompanied by sporadic blinding white flashes of lightning and ear-shattering peals of thunder, and in spite of being tired, he had trouble falling asleep. The bothersome noise from the outside and the events of the day, both the impressions from the archeological site and the time spent with the girl at the pool, made it difficult for him to relax. His thoughts were like the water in the pool in Uxmal after he'd dived into it and as if imitating it he kept tossing and turning in his bed.

At one point while doing this, as he faced the bed on his right, he became aware of the outline of his wife's body as she lay on it still, rolled into a ball under the sheet with her back turned toward him, and was overcome by an urge to make love.

It wasn't that he suddenly desired her personally or was planning to think about the girl while making love, but simply craved that feeling of peace and completeness the sexual act always brought him and wanted to experience it again. He really needed it badly just then.

He was afraid she was already asleep and would reject him, as she often did in similar situations, hating to be woken up in this fashion, but his urge was stronger than his fear and he decided to proceed with his plan.

He got quietly out of bed, got into hers, climbed in under the sheet beside her, and pressed himself against her body. She didn't show any signs of resistance and he proceeded to caress her, still encountering no opposition.

She didn't seem asleep and appeared to be willing to let him go further, which he did, in the end entering her from behind.

Now she started responding in a positive way to his movements so as to make them more effective, which excited him, and in the end his desire turned into a desire for her personally and he felt excited as he hadn't been for a long time.

He found the position they were in uncomfortable and not as effective as he wanted, and so disengaged himself, turned her over on her back, reentered her from the front, and proceeded with ever greater passion. She continued cooperating with him in her subdued way, which he found particularly arousing, his movements became quicker and more pronounced, and unexpectedly he found himself screaming with pleasure and after a few more afterthought-like motions let himself fall down on top of her. He hadn't felt pleasure like this for he didn't know how long.

After a while he slid off her and lay at her side, embracing her as best he could, without either of them saying a word.

Suddenly she got up and after explaining in a half-whisper she was going to wash up, went to the bathroom and shut the door.

After a few minutes she came out and on reaching the bed said there was no light in the bathroom. The power seemed to be out in the building, which must have been caused by the storm.

It was then that he noticed that the air conditioner which had been going almost nonstop since they had checked into the room was off and that outside the rain and thundering had stopped too. The room was eerily quiet.

She lay down next to him on his right, pressing against his side, a line parallel to the line of his body. He found the sensation pleasant but decided not to speak about it—speaking, it seemed, would affect his feeling in a negative way.

They lay like this, not stirring or speaking, and then unexpectedly she sat up and, turning to him and resting on her elbow, asked if he would like to have his face painted.

Instantly he became alive—she hadn't done it for years and he thought it would be wonderful. He recalled how she had done it first on Cape Cod and what beautiful feelings and images it had evoked in him then, and smiling in the darkness said in a loud voice that, yes, he did, and that it would be wonderful.

He adopted a more comfortable position for her and she sat up, turned further right, leaned over him, and began running the fingers of her left hand over his eyebrows, forehead, nose, lips, chin, and jaws as she had done it in the past.

Darkness was encroaching too much on his mind and the curves and surfaces he imagined being created by her were black and not white, but still the feel of her fingers on his face relaxed him and even before she had finished he fell asleep.

12

_____

He dreamed black empty dreams as his thoughts had been before he fell asleep, sleeping for at least an hour, because when he woke up it was hot in the room and he was covered with sweat. The air conditioner still wasn't working.

He lay still on his back as he'd been lying while falling asleep, and after a few seconds, having taken his bearings, realized his wife wasn't at his side.

It had been uncomfortable for the two of them lying squeezed together in the narrow bed and he figured she had moved over to his.

He turned his head left and saw that that's what it was—she lay curled up into a ball on her side, her back turned to him, a mirror image of what she had looked like when he saw her earlier from his bed.

He turned his head back and, still feeling sweat ooze out of his body, after a while, fell asleep, lulled by it as he'd been lulled by his wife's fingers earlier.

For a long time he walked through a vast black empty space until in the end he had the following dream.

He's somewhere in the tropics next to a wall that encloses a wide open area full of machinery designed for digging up ground and moving it around—bulldozers, excavators, drilling machines, conveyors, heavy trucks, and so forth. The sight reminds him of the movie *King Solomon's Mines* he saw as a teenager, although physically there's no resemblance between the former and the latter. It must be the word "mines" that links the two together.

He appears to be standing on a little hill—or a mound of earth more properly—because the wall is tall but he can see over it. He hasn't looked in the back but feels there's a jungle behind him—a dense forest of tall thick tropical trees. He imagines their roots and creepers that grow on them to look like giant twisting snakes—pythons. This must be another element that links his dream to the movie.

In the middle of the open area there's a huge conical mound of crushed stone with a conveyor belt on scaffolding leading to its top. This is where the excavated material is being piled up.

The conveyor isn't running at the moment and none of the other equipment is being operated but there are tall, strange-looking figures moving about between the latter. They walk on their hind legs and have arms like people but also something thick and long behind them that drags on the ground, supporting them, looking like big reptile tails.

He is puzzled by this, looks closer, and decides that this is what those strange things are—reptile tails. The creatures aren't people but giant iguanas that walk on their hind legs! They are the ones who are operating all this machinery and who are in charge of the site.

Something about them scares him—they are creatures who are not well-disposed toward humans. They make him think of the extraterrestrials described in H. G. Wells' *The War of the Worlds* which he had also read as a teenager.

What are they doing? He thinks. What is all the digging for? And then he realizes there's something round and dark on the ground visible behind the base of the conical mound—a hole. The iguanas are digging a hole in the ground which is to be like the holes—cenotes—the Maya used to throw sacrificial victims in. They'll be throwing people into it once they are done.

He feels endangered now and thinks of fleeing but can't tear his eyes away from the sight. There's something fascinating about being in danger.

It seemed to him at first the iguanas were moving about aimlessly but realizes now that that's not true. They seem to be busy with the equipment—inspecting and repairing it to make sure it works. This must be their lunchtime break—they have finished eating and are getting their equipment ready for use. Soon they'll start working.

At first he was seeing everything from afar but suddenly things are very close up. There's a big bulldozer right on the other side of the wall with an iguana moving around it, checking it here and there. It is no more than five feet away from him.

He feels really scared now and wants to run away, but something seems to be pressing against his back like a wall. What he had thought to be trees growing behind him is apparently a solid wall. It is the wall of the edge of jungle.

The iguana has gotten even closer now. He could touch it with his hand if he were to reach out. This is really scary. What will happen if it turns its head and sees him?

Will it grab him and throw him into the hole—that is, take him over to the other iguanas to be thrown into the hole? The prospect is terrifying.

At that moment in fact the iguana turns left and stops. A big, dark, flappy dewlap hangs down from its chin and its small round eye stares intensely out of its head. It is looking straight at him! It has recognized he's a human being and will grab him next!

Yuriy Tarnawsky

Terrified to the extreme he pushes against the wall at his back
and is ready to scream, No! but at that instant woke up.

He lay on his back drenched with sweat, fully uncovered, the
pillow wet under his head. It was dark in the room and the air
conditioner wasn't running. The power was still off.

Even though the phrase made no sense to him, he said to
himself, Those were the iguanas of heat.

13

The power didn't go on until shortly before dawn and he felt like a zombie sitting next to his wife in the bus on the way to Chichen Itza. The girl sat someplace in the back with her parents because they were late boarding the bus, but in the state he was in it didn't matter. She was on the bus and that was good enough for him.

The drive was longer than to Uxmal and went through more open country, the road—a perfectly straight gray line cutting through an expanse of solid green. As during the drive to Uxmal it was virtually flat, only occasionally rising for a brief stretch a couple dozen feet at the most above the even landscape. During the Uxmal excursion he learned that Yucatan was once a coral reef and was now bedrock of limestone with only a thin layer of soil over it. Because of that, all the rain that fell seeped through the porous stone to the bottom and there were no rivers or lakes there on the surface except only beneath the ground. The latter were the cenotes, which were sometimes joined by rivers running deep below.

More than halfway through the ride the bus sopped at a roadside cantina and the tour guide, this time a man, announced people were free to step out for a few minutes to use the bathroom, get a drink, or simply stretch their legs. About a dozen people got off.

He felt too tired to get off himself but as the girl brushed past him and he saw her walk down the aisle and go out the door, he decided to do it. She wore a navy-blue sweat shirt with a hood and white tennis shoes, but the same seductive denim shorts, and the sight of her slender hips undulating in them while she moved, as if beckoning him to come along, like an injection of a powerful drug woke him up in an instant and all of a sudden he was full of energy.

He let a respectable amount of time pass before proceeding and then told his wife he would get himself something to drink and asked if she wanted anything. She replied that she didn't, and he got off the bus, went into the cantina, and got in line. The girl was a couple of places before him, but as she stood with her back turned toward him, he didn't try making contact with her.

He didn't know what to get himself, but seeing what she selected, asked for the same.

It was a can of nectar of pear and as he stepped outside, he opened it, drank from it, and found it tasted delicious—sweet, and fragrant, and creamy. He'd never tried any pear drinks before and wondered why they weren't popular at home. This one tasted much better than apple juice.

The girl stood a few paces away from him, drinking, and he went up to her and remarked that the drink tasted great. He said he saw her pick it, tried it, and decided he'd made a good choice.

She loved it, she replied. You couldn't find it anywhere in Canada or the United States, but when she was in Mexico, she always drank it.

It tasted a bit like piña colada, he remarked, suddenly noticing the similarity.

He was right, she laughed. She hadn't realized it, but the two did taste similar. That's why she liked them. She liked sweet things.

Just things? Not people? He probed jokingly.

People too, of course, she laughed. Everything that's sweet.

Men? He pressed on. Sweet like him?

Yes, she laughed again. Especially sweet men, and after a brief pause added that she liked him.

He realized the conversation was getting out of hand and decided to cut it short, taking a long sip out of the can. Just then the tour guide appeared from somewhere and asked everyone to board the bus. It was getting late and they had to get going. They still had a little way to go.

He and the girl quickly finished their drinks, threw their cans into a waste container, and got on the bus.

He was elated. Things were going better than he'd expected. He didn't know where all this was leading to and how it was going to end, but it was moving in the right direction. There was no point in his worrying. No matter what happened he was sure everything would turn out well in the end.

Within half an hour they were in Chichen Itza.

The site was enormous, much bigger than Uxmal and much better restored. The ground in it was perfectly flat and was overgrown with thick, closely-cropped grass, which made it look like a giant table covered with freshly-ironed green cloth on which huge structures of stone had been arranged according to some obscure, complex principle.

There was the Pyramid of Kukulkan—Plumed Serpent, the legendary Maya deity—also known as El Castillo—the Castle— fully restored, with its base square like in Egyptian pyramids but with nine ever decreasing tiers of equal height standing for the nine levels of the underworld and stairs on each side leading to a temple at the top in which victims were sacrificed, the Temple of the Warriors with the Chacmool figure looking like a bench you could sit on but which actually served as the altar on which the freshly removed hearts of victims were placed in sacrifice, the nearby Hall of Thousand Columns, which looked especially interesting because its roof was missing, the Wall of Skulls along a platform, on top of which once stood stakes with heads of sacrificial victims impaled on them, the vast Sacred Ball Court with a temple in one corner, flanked by two tall walls with a stone ring in the center of each, through which the solid rubber ball used in the game had to pass for scoring, a few other smaller structures, and finally the Sacred Cenote, a man-made, open-air cenote a few dozen feet below ground level, into which sacrificial victims were thrown to propitiate the rain god Chac in times of drought.

His elation had turned to calmness. While their group was shown around the site, the guide commenting on what they were visiting, he saw the girl now close up, now far away among other people, but it didn't matter where she was. Even more than in Uxmal, he was certain something was going to develop between them. The way she'd acted that morning at the pool in Merida, and then at the one in Uxmal, and especially at the cantina stop on the way to Chichen Itza, had to mean something. There was no doubt she liked him. She openly said she did. She couldn't have been lying. And now she never smiled at him when they exchanged glances or passed each other, and behaved as if they were strangers, which could only mean she was serious about him and didn't want anyone to know it. The best way to achieve this was to show indifference. He suspected she'd planned something out already. When they went back to Merida she would somehow manage to ask him to meet her in the city that night and then the real thing would happen. He didn't know what "the real thing" was nor how it would happen, but was sure it would happen and that it would be the very thing he wanted.

Calmness transferred also to his feeling about life. Ever since his teens he'd been haunted by the prospect of death. The awareness of it was with him every minute of his every waking hour and colored his every action. It was the primary reason for his choosing philosophy as a profession and for his specializing in Existentialism. But now an extraordinary thing had happened. The prospect of dying no longer bothered him. The presence of death was virtually everywhere you turned on the site. In the temple atop the pyramid the victim's chest was cut open with an obsidian knife, his still throbbing heart was ripped out, his body was cut up, and the pieces were thrown down to the mob below to be consumed in ritual ceremonies. Victims were sacrificed in similar fashion at the Temple of the Warriors with the Chacmool figure which was mentioned earlier. Skulls were impaled on stakes atop the platform above the Wall of Skulls as was also mentioned earlier. Members of the losing team were put to death. People were thrown into the Sacred Cenote to drown in it. All of this made death seem no longer frightening. It was common, and thus part of life, and therefore acceptable. The various ceremonies, grizzly as they were, were clearly popular. They wouldn't have continued if people didn't want them, and since they wanted them, it meant they liked them, and since they liked them, it meant they were in some sense beautiful.

Beautiful like the girl, like the blinding sparkles of her sapphire eyes, like her blond hair which in a splash of white water fell out of her swimming cap at the pool in Merida, like her fluid, beckoning hips, like her long legs sprouting out of the revealing denim shorts in two elegant shoots.... If loving her and being loved by her was part of life, then there was nothing wrong with death being part of it too.

The nervousness brought on by the dream with the iguanas he had during the night didn't quite leave him however. As they were being shown the Sacred Cenote, while walking along its edge, he thought he saw a giant snake—a python—crawling toward him and jumped aside, emitting a strange-sounding yelp, such as he had never made before. He saw instantly he'd made a mistake though—it was the root of a tree that had grown over a rock looking like a snake creeping over it—and blushed with embarrassment. His wife, who'd been facing the other way, turned around quickly and looked at him with an expression of terror in her round, bulging eyes. She'd been taking pictures as they went around the site and was holding her camera in her hands.

He laughed awkwardly and said, Look at that root. It looks just like a snake. It scared me.

Why don't you take a picture of it? He added. It looks creepy.

She relaxed and without saying a word positioned herself better, raised the camera, pressed it to her forehead, and after a few seconds he heard it click.

It sounded like some huge animal snapping its jaws.

14

They had lunch at a hotel restaurant in the nearby village of Pisté, as in Uxmal, in the shade of trees and at the side of a swimming pool. The girl and her parents weren't there. They said they knew a little place in the village they liked and would lunch there.

After lunch they all met at the site and visited the rest of the ruins, which were on the other side of the highway, the most notable structure among them being *El Caracol*—the Snail— also known as the Observatory because of its round shape and the function it served in the old days. After that people scattered and went to explore the site on their own.

On their way back they looked for taxicabs to see if any of them would take them to the cenote, but there were none around. It was beginning to look unlikely that they would make it there and his wife was visibly dejected. The gloom on her face and the way she moved about displaying a total lack of energy made it clear she was extremely disappointed they would be going home without visiting the well. Having never had much interest in seeing it he was happy to skip it but tried to cheer her up, saying they'd try again later and that perhaps the Koenigs would be able to help them.

They hadn't been to the temple at the top of the pyramid during the guided tour and decided to take a look at it.

On the way there they ran into the Koenigs, who decided to join them. They were going there themselves. Their daughter once again wasn't with them. She'd run into the American kids she met in Merida and would join them later. As to finding a taxi driver, they said they would try to see what they could do after they finished sightseeing. They knew some people in the village who might be able to help.

In the middle of the temple there was a big rounded altar-like stone over which victims were held when their hearts were torn out of their chest as again was mentioned earlier. From the temple a narrow staircase lead down into the pyramid to two chambers which sat on top of earlier pyramids over which the big one was built, one of them—the Hall of Offerings— housing a Chacmool figure with mother of pearl eyes, nails, and teeth, and the other one—the Hall of Sacrifices—the Red Jaguar, a red painted bench-like figure similar to the Chacmool, with ivory fangs and eyes and spots of green jade.

The rooms were cramped, hot, and damp, packed with people, and since he was mildly claustrophobic, he decided to leave almost as soon as they got there. His wife and the Koenigs stayed on.

After climbing up the stairs back to the temple, to do which he had to fight an endless stream of people who kept coming down like a file of ants on some important mission, he stepped outside and breathed freely. It was great to be out in the open, feel the fresh air in his lungs, and let his eyes feast on the vast vistas of the flat green land stretching uninterrupted all the way to the horizon. He was feeling again as he had while standing on top of the pyramid in Uxmal.

But at that instant he heard his name being called from somewhere below, Mister Kramer! Mister Kramer! Mister Kramer!

Confused, at first he couldn't figure out where the voice was coming from but eventually realized it was from directly below him, at the base of the pyramid, and when he looked there, saw it was the girl, who was standing in the company of two men, one young, blond, tall and slender, the other one older, dark, short and stocky, her head thrown back, waving at him. She'd taken off the navy-blue sweat shirt with the hood earlier, when they got off the bus, and it hung draped over the shoulder bag she carried, and wore the white-on-white embroidered Mexican shirt she'd had underneath.

When she saw that he had noticed her, she stopped waiving and, climbing up a couple of steps, called out to him, asking if her parents were with them.

He heard her fine, but decided to descend a few steps himself so as to hear her better. Something bothered him as he was doing it and as he thought about it he realized it was the fact she was referring to him by his last name. Until then she'd always addressed him by his first. That seemed to point to something negative.

For a moment he thought that at least she should have called him "doctor" or "professor" but pushed the thought out of his mind as silly, and when he stopped and she asked him again if her parents were with him, he replied that they were— together with his wife in the inner chambers.

Would he be so kind then, she went on, to tell them she wouldn't be taking the bus back to Merida but would go right now with Brian—she turned toward and pointed at the younger man—in his car?

He was stunned. It was as if he was a mirror hanging on the wall which was suddenly hit by something hard, making it shatter and fall in pieces to the floor, exposing the bare surface underneath. The new himself he'd started to construct in Uxmal and felt he'd finished just an hour or two earlier literally a few dozen paces away was gone and in its place there was nothing.

Desperate, not wanting to accept what'd happened, as if thinking he could undo the meaning of her words, he descended a few more steps and called out to her in a desperate voice, But will they let you? They won't be worried? You can't do that!

It'll be alright, she called back, smiling and waving her hand. They won't mind. They know Brian. They've just met him. It'll be fine.

I'll meet them at the hotel, she continued. Tell them I'll be there for supper.

OK? She concluded.

He said nothing, staring at her in disbelief. His last drop of hope was gone. He'd tried to change her mind about going away with the boy and had failed. She would go away after all and he would be left alone.

And Mister Kramer, she went on, interrupting his thoughts. You were looking for someone to take you to that cenote.... This man here—she turned to the older man, pointing at him—he'll take you there. He knows where Pozo del Diablo is.

Have a great time. Byyye! She yelled cheerfully, once more waving her hand at him, climbed down to the ground, and walked off with the younger man in the direction out of the site.

He watched them walk for a few seconds, holding hands, their slim bodies swaying gracefully like underwater weeds in a gentle current, and then turned his head forward. He wasn't aware of what his eyes were seeing. The bare spot on the wall was gone and in its place was his old familiar self. The new himself he thought he'd created was gone for good. It had never existed but had been an illusion, something he'd merely wanted to be. He'd known it all along. How could have anything remotely meaningful developed between him, a married man in his forties, and a girl who wasn't even sixteen?! He was Walter Kramer, Professor of philosophy at a small Northeastern college who specialized in Existentialism, he'd been married to Greta Kraus for almost twenty years, and had come to Mexico to see the archeological sites around Merida and the cenote called Pozo del Diablo or Devil's Well his wife was set on seeing. The driver who would take them there was waiting below.

15

The man was middle-aged, not so much stocky as chubby, had thick, spiky jet-black hair, oddly enough was named Walter, and spoke decent English. He'd lived for a number of years working in the States, in Chicago, saved up some money, came back, bought himself a car, and made his living now as a taxi driver. He said in Mexico they called him "Vahlter," but "Walter"—he pronounced it "Guolter"— would be fine if that was what they preferred. That's what they had called him in the US. He said the trip would take close to a couple of hours, so they wouldn't be able to make it to the bus, but he would drive them back to the hotel. The price he quoted was not insignificant, but they agreed to it. It was their only chance to see the well.

The Koenigs agreed to let the tour guide know they weren't coming. As to the girl's going off with the boy, they didn't seem to be upset about it. Apparently such a thing wasn't unusual with her. This made him feel better about what'd happened. The mores of her generation were not those of his. Even if, unlikely as it was, something was going to develop between him and her, sooner or later it would have come apart and would have done it badly. It was better the whole thing ended as it did.

The cenote was in the direction to Valladolid, the man said, opposite from that to Merida, and off the main highway. Few people visited it, as it wasn't well-known, so it was no wonder drivers in Merida didn't know about it. Not even all the local drivers did. He was having a beer in the cantina, the girl was there with the boy, they started talking, and when she learned he drove a taxi, she asked him about the well. She said friends of her parents were looking for someone to take them there. So that's how she found him.

About twenty minutes after they left, the sky got dark and it began to thunder. Lightning could be seen all around, but far away in the distance. Blinding-white bolts of fire were shooting down from the black sky, thick and furry like roots of trees, such as he'd never seen before. Those he'd seen back home were puny in comparison. He concluded that it appeared as though hot climate had the same stimulating effect on lightning flashes as on plants.

Soon after that it started raining. The rain got progressively stronger and stronger and eventually it was coming down so hard they had to stop. There was a river flowing down the windshield and you couldn't see even a few inches ahead. They sat in the car with the windows rolled up, seemingly submerged in water, deafened by the incessant hammering of raindrops on the roof.

But just as suddenly as the storm came, it was gone, the sky cleared, and the sun came out. The air was fresh and clear like a newly-washed window pane.

They had to wait a while for the water on the road to recede, but eventually resumed their drive.

After driving for some time they turned left off the main highway onto a smaller road, drove along it some more, turned right off it onto an unpaved road, drove along it a little longer, and stopped. The driver killed the engine and started to get out.

They were there.

The driver got out first and then his wife. They'd been sitting in the back seat, he on the left and she on the right, and she went around the back of the car to join the driver. Apparently it was easier for her to get to him that way. As he heard her go past him in the back he imagined her seeing him through the rear window, his head, neck, and shoulders, and for some reason thought they would look to her like pieces of meat laid out for display in a butcher shop window.

He found the image unpleasant, pushed it out of his mind, hastily opened the door, shut it, and stepped forward, barring her way.

She wanted to let him go first, putting her hand on his arm, but he resisted her, put his hand instead on her shoulder, and guided her past him, noticing at the last minute her face looked flushed, which surprised him, since it'd been comfortable in the car with the window open and the air rushing in.

The driver was waiting for them, turned in their direction.

She obeyed him, walked forward, and as the driver turned around and began walking, she followed him, eventually catching up. He, in turn, followed her.

The road was narrow, hemmed in on both sides by bushes and tall grass. There were no cars or motorcycles visible anywhere and he observed they would be all alone.

Some twenty or thirty yards ahead he noticed the tops of trees rising above the bushes and concluded that was the hillock Walter Kaufman had talked about and the trees were the ones whose roots he'd seen in the picture. The cenote was under it.

The ground and the vegetation around him looked dry as if it hadn't rained there at all, but he was sure it had and that the water had merely soaked into the porous rock as it was said it always did and had already evaporated off the leaves and grass. The sun was shining and it felt hot.

He moved along the path, his eyes on the driver and his wife, who walked now next to each other, the backs of their heads tilting from side to side in rhythm with their walk like eyeless faces capable of seeing, for some reason trying to get a better look at him. There seemed to be something evil in them wanting to do it.

For a moment or two he had a feeling he was being reminded of a country road he once walked but he couldn't tell what road it was and what was reminding him of it, and so he pushed the thought out of his mind.

It'd been dead still all around until then, but suddenly he heard a faint chirping of a cricket somewhere nearby. It seemed as if it was doing it for the first time since the rain stopped, testing timidly if the ridges on its shell and its legs still worked. The sound was tentative and tremulous and made him think it was chills running up his spine as he had felt about the ripples on the surface of the water in the swimming pool in Uxmal almost exactly twenty-four hours earlier.

A checklist of JEF titles

☐ 0   *Projections* by Eckhard Gerdes

☐ 2   *Ring in a River* by Eckhard Gerdes

☐ 3   *The Darkness Starts Up Where You Stand*
        by Arthur Winfield Knight

☐ 4   *Belighted Fiction*

☐ 5   *Othello Blues* by Harold Jaffe

☐ 9   *Recto & Verso: A Work of Asemism and Pareidolia*
        by Dominic Ward & Eckhard Gerdes (Fridge Magnet Edition)

☐ 9B   *Recto & Verso: A Work of Asemism and Pareidolia*
        by Dominic Ward & Eckhard Gerdes (Trade Edition)

☐ 11   *Sore Eel Cheese* by The Flakxus Group (Limited Edition of 25)

☐ 14   *Writing Pictures: Case Studies in Photographic Criticism 1983-2012*
        by James R. Hugunin

☐ 15   *Wreck and Ruin: Photography, Temporality, and World (Dis)order*
        by James R. Hugunin

☐ 17   *John Barth, Bearded Bards & Splitting Hairs*

☐ 18   *99 Waves* by Persis Gerdes

☐ 23   *The Laugh that Laughs at the Laugh: Writing from and about the
        Pen Man, Raymond Federman*

☐ 24   *A-Way with it!: Contemporary Innovative Fiction*

☐ 28   *Paris 60* by Harold Jaffe

☐ 29   *The Literary Terrorism of Harold Jaffe*

☐ 33   *Apostrophe/Parenthesis* by Frederick Mark Kramer

☐ 34   *Journal of Experimental Fiction 34: Foremost Fiction: A Report
        from the Front Lines*

☐ 35   *Journal of Experimental Fiction 35*

☐ 36   *Scuff Mud* (cd)

☐ 37   *Bizarro Fiction: Journal of Experimental Fiction 37*

☐ 38   *ATTOHO #1* (cd-r)

☐ 39   *Journal of Experimental Fiction 39*

☐ 40   *Ambiguity* by Frederick Mark Kramer

☐ 41   *Prism and Graded Monotony* by Dominic Ward

☐ 42   *Short Tails* by Yuriy Tarnawsky

☐ 43   *Something Is Crook in Middlebrook* by James R. Hugunin

☐ 44   *Xanthous Mermaid Mechanics* by Brion Poloncic

☐ 45   *OD: Docufictions* by Harold Jaffe

☐ 46   *How to Break Article Noun* by Carolyn Chun

☐ 47   *Collected Stort Shories* by Eric Belgum

☐ 48   *What Is Art?* by Norman Conquest

☐ 49   *Don't Sing Aloha When I Go* by Robert Casella

☐ 50   *Journal of Experimental Fiction 50*

☐ 51   *Oppression for the Heaven of It* by Moore Bowen
☐ 52   *Elder Physics* by James R. Hugunin
☐ 53.1   *Like Blood in Water: Five Mininovels (The Placebo Effect Trilogy #1)* by Yuriy Tarnawsky
☐ 53.2   *The Future of Giraffes: Five Mininovels (The Placebo Effect Trilogy #2)* by Yuriy Tarnawsky
☐ 53.3   *View of Delft: Five Mininovels (The PlaceboEffect Trilogy #3)* by Yuriy Tarnawsky
☐ 54   *You Are Make Very Important Bathtime* by David Moscovich
☐ 55   *Minnows: A Shattered Novel* by Jønathan Lyons
☐ 56   *Meanwhile* by Frederick Mark Kramer
☐ 58A   *Tar Spackled Banner* by James R. Hugunin
☐ 58B   *Return to Circa '96* by Bob Sawatzki
☐ 60   *Case X* by James R. Hugunin
☐ 61   *Naked Lunch at Tiffany's* by Derek Pell
☐ 62   *Tangled in Motion* by Jane L. Carman
☐ 64   *The Hunter* by Dominic Ward
☐ 65   *A Little Story about Maurice Ravel* by Conger Beasley, Jr.
☐ 66   *Psychedelic Everest* by Brion Poloncic
☐ 67   *Between the Legs* by Kate Horsley
☐ 68   *Claim to Oblivion: Selected Essays and Interviews* by Yuriy Tarnawsky
☐ 69   *Passions and Shadows or Shadows and Passions* by Frederick Mark Kramer
☐ 70   *Afterimage: Critical Essays on Photography* by James R. Hugunin
☐ 71   *Goosestep* by Harold Jaffe
☐ 72   *Science Fiction: A Poem!* by Robin Wyatt Dunne
☐ 73   *Offbeat/Quirky*
☐ 74   *Mouth* by Charles Hood
☐ 75   *Q↔A* by James R. Hugunin
☐ 76   *Literary Yoga* by Yuriy Tarnawsky
☐ 77   *Experimental Literature: A Collection of Statements* edited by Jeffrey R. Di Leo and Warren Motte
☐ 78   *The Skrat Prize Memorial Anthology* by R.M. Strauss
☐ 79   *Black Scat Books: A Bibliography 2012 – 2018* compiled by Grace Murray
☐ 80   *Mememo* by James R. Hugunin
☐ 81   *Porn-anti-Porn* by Harold Jaffe
☐ 82   *Understanding Franklin Thompson* by Jim Meirose
☐ 83   *Warm Arctic Nights* by Yuriy Tarnawsky
☐ 84   *The Iguanas of Heat* by Yuriy Tarnawsky

JEF

Journal of
Experimental
Fiction